BAD MOON RISING

DOG RIVER WOLFPACK: BOOK ONE

KIMBRA SWAIN

Kimbra Swain
Bad Moon Rising: Dog River Wolfpack, Book One

ASIN: B0828N448K

Kimbra Swain / Crimson Sun Press, LLC
kimbraswain@gmail.com
crimsonsunpress@gmail.com

Ebook Cover by: Fantasia Cover Design: Sharon Lipman
Formatting by: Crimson Sun Graphics
Editing by Carol Tietsworth: https://www.facebook.com/Editing-by-Carol-Tietsworth-328303247526664/

ONE

WHEN SHE STEPPED into my office, my heart lurched at seeing her again after the way our first two meetings had gone. However, she clearly wasn't here for *that* this time.

"Lyra, is everything okay?" I asked as my senses forewarned me of her mood. I could smell her instability.

She shifted her weight, sighing deeply. Opening her mouth to speak, regret flowed from her dark blue eyes. She hated me. Hated what had happened between us. That would explain a lot, actually. She had helped me search for Rory and Soraya, but we'd barely spoken.

Lyra Rochon was the Alpha female of the Dog River Wolfpack just south of Steelshore. She ran the pack with her two aunts, who were the matriarchs.

"I need your help," she mumbled.

Life had taught me to be guarded. Her disappearance and lack of responses to messages and calls had reinforced that principle. I'd enjoyed our time together more than I should have.

Grace and Levi sent me here to help the supernaturals

in this city. Even though Lyra wasn't technically from Steelshore, she and her sister lived close enough. But I didn't dare lower my guard.

"What can I do for you?" I asked, remaining seated behind my desk.

"Wow. I didn't expect such coldness. Not from you," she fired at me.

"Why not? I tried contacting you. You made it very clear that you weren't interested in talking to me again," I fired back.

"Perhaps I had more important things going on than responding to a mistake!" she exclaimed. "I should never have come back here."

Turning on her heel, she marched toward the door. Cursing me under her breath where I could hear it, I waited for her to change her mind. I wasn't going to chase her after she'd ghosted me.

Looking back over her shoulder, the fire subsided in her eyes. Her shoulders slumped. Raising her hands to her hips, she stared at the floor.

Whatever had brought her here was important. More important than her pride, which we both had in abundance. For that reason and a twinge of curiosity, I apologized.

"Forgive me. This is not about us, is it? What can I do to help you?" I relented.

Her voice was just above a whisper. "No, it's not about us. It's about my family."

Lyra took care of her younger sister, Tinley, after their parents were killed in an invasion into their territory. Lyra's pack had retained control over the Dog River region, but she had lost both parents in the process. Her father was the Alpha with no male heir. However, their pack had always been guided by her great aunts, the matriarchs of the pack. They put Lyra in charge. She struggled to retain control which she hadn't told me. However, after one night in bed, I knew. She fought me for control. I let her have it. It was what she needed.

Two nights. Then silence.

In the end, I knew it didn't matter that I had allowed her to take the lead. She had given me more than she had ever intended. She left me with the wanting desire to have someone of my own. To share a life. It didn't have to be her, but it would have been nice to have another wolf who understood the struggles of an Alpha. I couldn't call myself an Alpha, but it still flowed through my veins.

"Nick, another pack is moving into the region. There is discord in my pack. They are losing faith in my leadership abilities. I need an Alpha," she whimpered.

"I'm not an Alpha. Besides you *are* an Alpha," I responded quickly.

"Just because you renounced it, doesn't mean it isn't still in you!" she growled.

"I can't lead your pack," I said.

"You won't. It's mine, but I need back-up," she said.

"I'll call Mark. He can send down some fighters to help protect the pack," I responded.

"No outsiders!" she exclaimed.

Her emotions teetered from high to low like a squeaky see-saw.

"It wouldn't be permanent. The Shady Grove pack is trained for this kind of thing. We help shifters all over the country. Not just wolves. They would be under your control," I said.

She stomped back across the room in her killer heel boots and leaned over my desk. Her eyes flashed bright yellow with the animal inside of her. I'd seen that flash in bed.

"I didn't ask for the Shady Grove pack. I asked for *you*, but you are a coward. You think because you lost a hand that you can't lead. That no one but your little task force here will listen to you. Get over yourself, Dominick. Are you going to help me or not?" Her voice dripped with fire. The fire I'd come to associate with strong, stubborn southern women.

Grace.

Wynonna.

Lyra.

Fuck me.

"Let me grab my jacket."

TWO

WHILE IN SHADY GROVE, I joined Grace and Levi Rearden as they took the rule of the Winter Realm from her uncle. Our first confrontation with him didn't go well, and I lost a hand in the process. I'd saved her life, and I'd do it again, but losing my hand scared the shit out of me. As a wolf shifter, I couldn't function without a paw. I couldn't run. I'd be the weakest of the pack. Even with my past and all the crap I'd faced as a young man, nothing devastated me more than looking at a stump.

Levi helped me learn to pull on the fairy side of me to glamour myself a hand. Grace claimed the success as her stubbornness, but it was Levi who showed me the way. He was like a brother to me. We were both half-fairy. My mother slept with my father, an Alpha wolf, to produce an heir. Faeborn. I should have been called Outcast. I didn't turn out to be the Alpha my father wanted, nor did the pack accept me. Had I stayed the pack would have killed me. I ran, but in running, I had always felt like a coward. My father and his wife, Regina, died in the aftermath, and the entire Whiskey Chitto Pack was killed or incorporated into the Oberlin pack.

Along the way, I met Sullivan and Suzanna. Sully and Suzi. My siblings. We found out that we had the same fairy-meddling mother who also killed their father and destroyed the hierarchy of the Houma pack. We weren't sure, but the best we could tell, she controlled more than half the packs in Louisiana. Reuben, Suzi's mate, took her and his closest family to Shady Grove. We pushed them through the processing center, because Araxia, my mother, was coming after them. Either you followed her, or you died.

Sully and I had told Levi all about it once everything calmed down after the war. He and Grace were doing everything they could in the Otherworld to track the woman who was trafficking captured fairies and selling them on the black market. We'd come up with nothing concrete except for a base of operations in Steelshore. We didn't even know why or what she was getting in return. I knew that it wasn't good, whatever it was.

So, while Sully roamed through the southern states trying to gather information, I went to Steelshore with a task force, hoping to find my mother. Wynonna Riggs, Levi and Grace's daughter, went with me. It had been our intention from the beginning to turn the operations there over to her, then move me back to Birmingham to head up the Fairy Bureau of Investigations there. I would have access to all fairies going to and from the Otherworld. Grace and Levi had even powered a new portal there to keep the influx of fairies from going through Shady Grove which had become overpopulated.

Winnie proved to us that she could handle the operations in Steelshore. I'd agreed to stay a little longer and oversee her progress, but Lyra showed up at my door asking for help. I'd met Lyra Rochon in a rinky-dink bar just outside of Steelshore. One thing led to another, and we slept together. That's when we both realized we were wolves.

At first, it scared the hell out of me, considering the wolves of the south were partially populated by my mother. Or so it seemed, but Lyra proved to be a purebred wolf. Her family had ruled the Dog River area south of Steelshore since the French settled in Steelshore. We talked briefly about wolves, packs, and life before she left me in the hotel room without a way to contact her.

The next time it happened, she found me. She'd somehow tracked me to the apartment where I lived, with Wynonna next door. I was sure our activities disturbed the neighbors. I persuaded Lyra to give me her number, but she made me promise to never use it. That night, I followed her back to Dog River and found out more about her than she had ever told me.

Lyra was a rare Alpha female. Her pack had always respected the female line of Alphas whereas most packs bred the females out of existence. The early packs in America had barbaric ways that evolved over the years, but the Dog River pack cherished their Alpha women. Her aunts, Agatha and Eulalie Rochon ran the pack. Even when Lyra's father, the previous Alpha, lived, the Aunts ran the pack. Both looked like they had lived over a century, and to my knowledge, they might have. Sometimes wolves can have extremely prolonged lives.

To avoid getting caught, I left Dog River, but Lyra stayed a part of me. I loathed the fact that she owned a part of me. I loved that I'd given it to her without even noticing. But I'd seen her return home to the arms of another man. Just before I left her town, I asked one too many questions.

It was the last one that got me in trouble, because then she found out that I was there.

The man I'd seen her embrace was Cortland DuChien, the man everyone expected her to marry. I hated him immediately although I had no reason for it. No reason except for the wolf inside of me had tethered itself to Lyra. She was the only wolf I'd ever slept with. No wonder I craved her.

My phone rang the next day, and Lyra cussed me in English then she cussed me in a mix of French and something else I'd later learn was Creole. She accused me of stalking among other unsavory things, and I decided to let her go. I couldn't tarnish the name of the King and Queen, because I had an obsessive streak over an overbearing, she-wolf.

When I talked to Sully about it, he had some good advice once he finished making fun of me.

"Have you ever slept with another wolf?" he asked.

He had a point. I'd only slept with humans. I feared the connection of my wolf with another, and when it happened with Lyra, I hadn't been going for that.

"No."

"You are just inexperienced."

"I am not inexperienced. Don't make me prove it."

"Incestuous bastard."

"No, you moron, I'd make you watch."

"Oh, really?"

"Sully!" My brother had hit on me multiple times before we realized we were siblings. He'd even kissed me to prove a point. It didn't appall me then, but it did now. It was something we *never* talked about with anyone else.

"You are inexperienced with wolves, and you've denied that connection to your own inner animal that is latched onto her. The best thing you can do is go find a different wolf and sleep with her," he advised.

However, there was no time for that with the Sanhedrin standing in our way every time we tried to help the fairies who were being sold on the black market. Then came the war between the Siren and the Mermaid that delayed our efforts. I hadn't had time to think about another wolf, much less find one.

"What are you thinking about?" she asked as she drove her Jeep south out of town.

"My brother," I said, trying not to elaborate.

"Is he Faeborn too?" she asked with disdain.

"Yes," I said. "He could help us. I can call him. He's over in Louisiana doing some leg work for the crown."

"I'm taking you into wolf territory. Don't bring your fairy shit to us. If that is going to be a problem, you've got to go back. I'll lose everything, and that will be the end of it," she said.

"What exactly is going on?" I asked. I supposed I should have made her be more specific when I agreed to help her.

"A Mississippi pack has taken over three packs in the lower Alabama area. They are pushing toward us. A couple of men showed up this afternoon. They flat out refused to speak to me about pack business. It was two scouting members from that pack," she said.

She'd set a fire alarm off in my head. "Were they Faeborn?" I asked, hoping she would say no.

"How am I supposed to know that?" she sassed back.

"Look, Lyra. You could drop the fucking attitude for five minutes. I'm in the car. I left my entire team to come and help you. Help me, help you."

Her jaw flexed under the flawless skin of her cheek. Then a tear rolled over it. I should have held my tongue.

She waited until she could speak before she replied. "Thank you, Nick for coming. This might be a terrible idea, but if they won't talk to me, I'm betting they will talk to you. I don't trust anyone in my own pack." That alarmed me. Why wouldn't she trust her own pack?

"What about Cortland DuChein?" I tried to ask it without sounding too jealous.

"Cort doesn't have an Alpha bone in his body. They would smell his weakness. I need someone who smells of strength. If I stepped out there with him, they would kill him. And while I'm not in love with Cort, he is my best friend."

"I smell like strength?"

"You smell like Alpha, despite your idea that you aren't one anymore. That smell doesn't go away. That blood flows through your veins like it does mine."

"Is that how you found me the second time?" I asked.

"Partially. I have friends in Steelshore. They knew where to find you."

"One of those friends wouldn't happen to be a Vampirate would he?"

"Who, Seamus?"

"Are there others?"

"Not recently. In the past there were, but he's a survivor. He adapts to the changing times. And yes, Seamus told me where to find you."

I didn't know whether to thank the vampirate or curse him. However, I trusted Seamus. He'd proven his loyalty to our cause more than once. I'd called him right before I left Winnie, and he promised to keep an eye on her for me. I wondered what Grace would think of it, but I didn't care. I mean, I did, because she would rip me a new one if something happened to her daughter, but Seamus adored Winnie. I knew he wouldn't let anything happen to her while I sorted things out for Lyra. But the way she talked; it wasn't going to get sorted out quickly.

"These men, did they demand anything?"

"Just to prepare for our new Alpha who would arrive in a couple of days," she said. "No one is taking my pack."

"I agree. No one is taking it. I'll stand with you. Just tell me what you need from me. Are we pretending to be together? I could stand behind you and support you, but if these guys are as deadly as you think, I don't think that's going to work."

Her jaw flexed again. She needed to work out her aggression and anxiety. Too bad she's sworn off of that with me. I was sure I could fix her up.

"Stop leering at me."

"I wasn't."

"Nick, it's not going to happen again. We need to pretend to be together. You smell like an Alpha. So, that means I smell like you since we've been together. Even Cort says I don't smell the same."

"Wait? What?"

"Cort says I smell differently."

"Like me?"

"I don't know if it is you or not. I can't smell it, but he's not the only one that noticed."

"Who else noticed?"

She sighed. "Everyone."

THREE

LYRA LIVED along the Dog River in a small river house that had survived several hurricanes. She shared the house with her sister, Tinley. I hadn't met her, but Lyra had talked about her a little. When we pulled up in the drive, Lyra gave me instructions. I figured that I'd be getting ordered around for however long I was here. Might as well start now.

"Tinley is probably asleep. There are only two bedrooms in this house, and I don't want her finding you on the couch in the morning. It's best if you sleep in my room. I'll take the couch just for tonight, and then when I explain everything to her, she can sleep with me, and you can have her room," she said.

"I can sleep on the floor, Lyra. She can keep her bed," I said.

"She's not going to like you being in the house. She will be afraid of you."

"Why? Does she know about us?"

"Hell, no. She's just skittish in general."

"All right. What else?"

"Go easy on her, please. She's never shifted, and some in the pack question her position as my sister."

"And potential heir," I surmised.

"She won't ever lead this pack, but I want her kept safe and respected."

"Gotcha. I know you don't know me very well, but Lyra, I really am here to help you. My past revolves around this pack take-over shit, and I've got some bills to pay."

"You'll have to tell me about it sometime." The harshness in her voice had faded as if she believed me when I said that I was going to help. She'd come to me because she knew I would. I doubted she knew anything about my father and my mother's involvement with controlling the packs. I needed to see these enforcers that had showed up. Then, I would know what we were dealing with and how to protect the Dog River Pack.

We walked into the house, and Lyra stepped without making a noise. Her footsteps were light, and I followed to her bedroom. When we passed her sister's bedroom door, I could hear the soft sounds of her breathing. My Alpha senses told me immediately that she was small and needed to be protected.

Lyra's bedroom housed a queen-sized bed, a dresser, and a small wooden chair. I carried a duffel bag of clothes I'd hastily thrown together just before Lyra picked me up. I sat it gently on the floor.

"Is this okay?" she asked.

"It's fine. I can sleep on the floor, so you can stay in your bed," I whispered.

"No."

"You can't be in the same room with me?" I asked, lifting an eyebrow.

"Stop it!" she hissed. I'd hit that nail on the head. "Goodnight, Nick."

"Goodnight."

She left me standing in an unfamiliar room which was covered in her scent. I sat down on the bed, and moving around stirred up the smell even more. I couldn't do it. I'd be sleeping on the floor, because if I slept in that bed, it would be with a raging hard-on. My blue balls and I would be much better away from the reminder.

~

The floor provided little comfort for me, but I slept. When I woke up, I heard two quiet voices coming from the kitchen. The smell of pancakes filled the room, and my stomach groaned in approval. I didn't bother with a shirt but made sure I was wearing pants. Shirtless men were a norm in most packs. Of course, every pack was different.

As I moved down the hallway, their voices stopped. Turning the corner, my jaw dropped. Sitting at the small kitchen table, Tinley looked up at me with violet eyes and two-toned hair. The top was as dark as her sister's, but the bottom was bleached white. She looked nothing like her sister. In my peripheral vision, I saw Lyra's eyes widen. Something was off about her little sister, but I couldn't put my finger on it.

"Tinley, this is the rude man I was talking about. Nick, this is my sister," Lyra said.

"Hi," I said, suddenly feeling self-conscious and wishing I'd worn a shirt.

Tinley didn't speak. She smiled, then lowered her gaze to her plate of pancakes. "Sit down, you brute." Lyra slapped a plate of pancakes down at the table.

"You know, I should have grabbed a shirt," I said.

"Sit down," she demanded. I felt the Alpha pull of her command. My Alpha responded by making my pants tighter. "We've both seen shirtless men."

"Okay," I responded. "This looks wonderful."

"It's pretty good. Just eat and shut-up before you say something stupid," Lyra said, as she sat down across from me with her plate.

"Yes, ma'am." Tinley kept her eyes on her plate, but I saw her smile growing.

We ate in silence for a few minutes until Lyra spoke. "We've got to go see my aunts. They insisted that I take you to them when you got here. It was too late last night."

"The matriarchs?" I asked to clarify.

"Yes, they run the pack. Sort of. I mean, I'm the leader, but they dictate the important stuff," she explained. "They are eccentric." Tinley snorted. "Very eccentric."

"Okay. What do I need to know?"

Lyra cut her eyes to Tinley, then back to me. She shook her head. Tinley didn't know about the trouble which made her even more vulnerable. We needed help. I had to convince Lyra to allow me to call Sully to even see if Suzi and Rueben could come. I hadn't seen her pack, but if she didn't trust them, I had my own pack of friends that I trusted. People I'd give my life for, and if I asked them to protect Tinley or anyone else in this town, they'd do it.

"They live up the street. If I had to guess, I'd say they already knew you were here."

"I'll be on my best behavior."

"Your best behavior worries me just as much as all the other behaviors you have."

She never gave me an inch. Establishing her dominance. She could have it. For now.

"I look forward to showing you all of them."

She picked up her empty plate, then mine. "Tinley, eat!"

she demanded. The young girl let out a groan, but she put a bite in her mouth.

"How old are you, Tinley?" I asked.

"Eighteen," she replied. She looked no older than fifteen, maybe sixteen. I'd never guessed that this fragile looking creature was a woman. If those wolves came into this town, they would ruin her. I looked up to Lyra who winced. She knew it, too. I jumped up from the table, crossing the room to Lyra.

"Let me help you with the dishes," I offered.

"I've got it. You are a guest," she said.

"I'm pretty much family right now."

I laid my real hand on her arm, and she looked at me with pleading eyes. She never wanted to talk about things, but she had to for me to trust her. To protect her.

"Nick," she said with her eyes darting from me to Tinley.

"You have to let me call for help," I muttered.

"No."

I tightened my grip on her arm, and her nostrils flared. "Lyra. Her life depends on it."

"No." She jerked her arm away from me. "Go put on clothes. Something nice to meet my aunts."

I didn't verbally respond to her, but I obeyed her order. I knew if I went behind her back, she would never trust me again. If I didn't, wolves were going to die. I had to make a choice. While in her room getting dressed, I sent a simple text to Sully. I knew he'd understand.

FOUR

WE WALKED down the road together, hand in hand, with Tinley trailing behind us. I looked up into the sky where two extremely large ravens circled. The two birds were friends of mine. Malphas and Echo. They were servants of the Winter Queen, and my companions to help establish our presence in Steelshore. They were a rare form of fairy who were bonded. Echo was mute, but he could sign. He occasionally used his voice, but it was an audible telepathic thing. They had followed me from Steelshore, but I'd asked them to keep their distance. I'd find a way to talk to them. They must have had information for them to be hovering so close.

"They speak a lot of Cajun. So, if you miss something, I'll fill you in later," Lyra explained. She waved with her other hand to a woman who stood outside her house, staring at us. "Hey Mrs. Rachel, how're your boys?"

"They're fine," she replied.

"Dat's good," Lyra responded. Her speech pattern

slipped from the formal I was used to hearing to a more native slur.

The southern parts of Alabama were much like Louisiana in that the French, Spanish, African and Native American cultures mixed together. Steelshore claimed to have had the first Mardi Gras parade, not New Orleans. You'll find plenty of gumbo, etouffee, and jambalaya in the bayous of the area. The Cajun and Creole culture still thrived in some places. I'd heard the speech patterns before in Louisiana, and I knew a lot of their words. I would surprise Lyra with my understanding. It would be nice to one-up her on something.

"What do your aunts want to know about me?"

"Everything. They will be forward. They have no tact, and I'm preparing myself to be fully embarrassed."

"I look forward to that," I smirked. Tinley giggled behind us. "Tinley agrees."

"Don't make friends with her," Lyra warned.

"It's too late. She already likes me." Lyra cut her eyes from me back to Tinley. Her forehead wrinkled and her eyes narrowed at her sister. I was right. Tinley was fully on Team Nick.

"She will get over it when you leave."

I stopped walking, and Lyra pulled my hand to get me to move forward, but I refused. Tinley stopped close to us.

"This may take longer than you think. I will see it through."

"Stop being a fucking knight."

"Technically, I am one."

"This isn't Winter."

"And you need help. Look at my shining armor," I said with a wink. I brushed invisible dust from my shoulder.

"Could you be serious for just a little while?"

"I can be serious, but you told me we couldn't do *that*

anymore." Tinley put her hand over her mouth and looked down.

Lyra's upper lip twitched, and I saw her fangs. "Nick," she said through her teeth.

"Lyra," I mocked.

"Please don't make this any harder than it already is."

"I'm sure you don't want me to talk about hardness with your sister here."

Lyra threw her hands in the air in frustration. I held my hand out to Tinley. She grinned and took it. "I'd rather hold your hand anyway," I said to her.

"I'd like that," Tinley responded, taking my hand. Lyra stopped ranting when her sister placed her small hand in mine.

"Lead the way, Madam Alpha," I said.

Lyra rekindled her anger, spinning around to walk down the road. She looked over her shoulder at us. Tinley seemed content to hold my hand as we walked. My magic felt the magic in her. She wasn't Faeborn. She wasn't pure wolf either, but I had a pretty good idea what she was.

We walked up to a small yellow clapboard house. It featured a smallish porch with one rocking chair. An older woman with graying hair sat in the chair, rocking lazily. On the steps, another woman around the same age sat with a large steel wash basin between her legs. Her fingertips were purple from the peas she was shelling into the basin. Neither of them looked up when we approached.

A wreath hung on the front door that surprised me. A crescent moon made of dried vines with rosemary and sage stuck into it with chrysanthemum, dandelions, and clover filling the form. Three crystals hung from the bottom: amethyst, smoky quartz, and obsidian. The aunts had a wiccan friend that had protected their home.

"I smell him, Sister," the woman in the rocking chair said.

"As do I. He smells delectable," the other answered. They lifted their pale blue eyes to me.

"Lyra, child, you did not tell us that he was so handsome."

"Handsome isn't what we need," Lyra commented.

"I've found that handsome gets me a lot of things," I said.

"A quick wit," the one in the chair said.

"Very quick," the other answered.

"Dominick Meyer, these are my aunts. Eulalie Rochon in the chair, and this is Agatha Rochon," Lyra said, placing her hand on Agatha's shoulder. The woman patted it with affection.

"What other talents do you have, Mr. Meyer?" Eulalie asked. "And you may call me Eula and my sister, Aggie."

"Well, Eula, please call me Nick. And I can't tell you everything or you will bore of me too quickly," I said.

"He's too funny to be an Alpha," Aggie commented.

"Ah, humor is underrated," Eula responded.

"Your smell is on our Lyra," Aggie said.

I swallowed, and Lyra turned deep red. Tinley squeezed my hand. "I suppose it is," I replied.

"She needs a good smell on her," Eula said.

"Aunt Eula! Please," Lyra groaned.

"It's true. If I were younger, I'd let him coat me in that smell," Aggie said. Tinley turned her face into my arm, and I chuckled. I liked the aunts, especially because they made Lyra cringe with every word out of their mouths.

"Younger? You can't be older than forty. I like a little age on my women," I said.

"If I could still shift, I'd take you up on that," Aggie replied. "And I see our Tinley has taken to you. She senses your strength and gravitates to it. I suspect that is why Lyra found you attractive, too."

"It's been a long time since I was considered the heir of an Alpha. I was never a true Alpha in my own right. I'm a Beta now by choice," I said.

"Choice. That's the strength in you. You choose your destiny. You do not allow it to choose you," Eula said.

"Too bad your destiny will force you to choose something you thought you lost or never deserved. I smell your fairy blood," Aggie said.

"Yes, it is strong," Eula added.

"My mother was a Winter fairy," I confirmed.

"Being Faeborn doesn't make you any less a wolf," Aggie said.

"No, it doesn't," I agreed.

"It makes you a damn strong wolf," Eula said.

"And your hand," Aggie asked, pointing to my glamoured hand.

"Most can't tell the difference, but it's fully functional." I lifted my hand and flexed it to show them that it was as real as the one I had lost.

"Come inside and sit with us a while. We have things to discuss," Agatha said, as she tried to stand. Lyra helped her up, and I grabbed the basin of peas. Tinley took them from me with a smile and disappeared into the house. I followed the women inside and felt the ward as I crossed it. A very strong ward of protection.

The aunts sat down on a Victorian couch. I took a seat in an ornate chair. Just as Lyra started to sit in the one next to me, Eula clicked her tongue.

"What?" Lyra asked.

"We want to speak to him alone," Eula said.

"No," Lyra responded.

"Please do not make us undermine your authority in front of our guest," Aggie said.

Lyra snarled, then stomped out of the room like a child. It drove me wild. All of the things that went through my head would have shamed a lady of the night.

"She is still listening, but we did not want her in the room. She cannot reenter until we invite her," Eula explained.

"There is powerful magic in this house," I commented.

"Good. I'm glad you can feel it. Another benefit of being Faeborn," Aggie said, as she picked up two needles and yarn. Her weathered hands danced in rhythm producing links to something that would be warm and made with love.

"The threat to our pack isn't a surprise to us. As you suspect, we have a friend that warned us of the dark days ahead. She also told us that a man would arrive to help. She explained that he would be the outcast child of an Alpha and a fairy. She also said he would know our people in a unique way. How is that possible?" Eula asked.

"I grew up in Louisiana. This place reminds me of home," I said.

"You found a new home," Eula said.

"I found a new family. I can't say that I found a place I belong," I replied. She was dragging truths out of me that I wasn't prepared to admit.

"Perhaps that place is here," she suggested.

I looked to the door that Lyra had gone through and refused to allow myself to think of her as home. Aggie stopped knitting, and both women waited for me to respond.

"I'm here to help make your home safe. To keep Tinley safe. To help Lyra establish her rule," I said.

"You won't allow yourself to think about a future

because of the way your past has made you. Now is the time to define yourself by what is to come. Who you want to be."

"What if I don't know what I want to be?"

"What if you are just too afraid to admit it?" Eula asked.

Family. A real one. I didn't want to admit it. I had my responsibilities to Grace and Levi. To the Shady Grove pack. To my brother and sister. All of these things would come before what I wanted. I'd chosen to be Grace's knight. I'd chosen to accept my siblings. I'd chosen to get to the bottom of the fairy trafficking.

"You can do it all, Son," Aggie said.

"I like to take things one at a time."

"You'll never get anything done that way," Eula said.

"Maybe not."

We turned our attention to someone suddenly screaming outside. I stood up, and my claws extended.

"Oh," Aggie gasped.

Lyra ran into the room with Tinley. "You stay here," she said, pushing Tinley back.

"Come here, baby," Aggie said, and Tinley curled up next to her.

A hulking man ran inside. His eyes flashed with his wolf when he saw me and growled.

"Cort! Stand down!" Lyra ordered.

He took a step back but didn't retract his claws or fangs. "They are back. They are beating Landon Crosse down in front of Sally's restaurant," he said.

"Tinley stay here. Showtime, Alpha," Lyra said.

Cort sprinted ahead of us. Rounding the corner, we saw a crowd gathered outside a restaurant right next to the river. It had wooden picnic tables on a porch that surrounded it.

"Stop! Please stop!" a man begged. We heard blow after blow before we could get there.

Lyra pushed through the crowd, and I grabbed her arm. "Let me go!"

"Lyra, decide now. How are we doing this? You or me?" I asked.

I saw the pain and anger in her face. I could smell it in her sweat. "You. You go." I touched her cheek then bolted through the crowd to see two men holding a man, Landon Crosse, while another took punches at him. Blood dripped from his face and stained his blue t-shirt. It angered me, and when the man beating him went to land another blow, I stepped in front of it. His fist hit me in the chest, and I snarled in pain. But I'd done enough to shock him. The man stepped back and grinned.

"Well, this pack does have an Alpha," he laughed, shaking his hand.

"You will leave this town and not step foot in it again," I said.

"Or what? Do you think one Alpha is going to stop us?" he asked.

I reached out to my side holding my hand out to Lyra. She stepped forward and took it. "There are two here," I said.

"Forgive me if I'm not impressed," he said.

"How about three?" Sully asked as he stepped out of the crowd. Lyra squeezed my hand so tightly that I wanted to yelp in pain as her fingernails dug into my skin.

"A couple of outcasts and a female. I'm still not worried," the man said.

I lifted my free hand and called upon the power that Levi had taught me to tap into. I couldn't do much other than produce a snowball, but I hoped it would have the effect I needed.

"This *outcast* has the blessing of the Winter Queen, Gloriana," I said as the snow swirled above my hand.

"Nice trick, Loner. But the only wolf here that smells like you is her," he said, nodding to Lyra. "This isn't your pack, and they don't look like fighters to me."

"Try us," I said. A few of the wolves standing around us produced claws and fangs enough to convince him. "Leave. If you come back, I'll kill you."

"I can't wait until we meet again, Dominick Meyer," he said, then climbed into a pick-up with the other two men. They drove off in a cloud of dust. Two members of the pack helped Landon Crosse get to his feet.

"He knew your name," Lyra said. "And you called your brother!"

"Nice to meet you, Lyra. He did say you were a handful, but he never told me how beautiful you were," Sully said.

"Really?" I groaned at Sully, then turned back to Lyra. "I don't know how he knew my name."

"I do," Sully said.

"Yeah, how?"

"His name is Rocco Davis. He's Creed Davis' son," Sully said.

"Fucking hell," I muttered.

FIVE

SULLY and I followed a very angry Lyra back to her house. She'd called her aunts to let them know the crisis was averted for now.

"You didn't tell her I was coming," Sully said.

"No, I didn't."

"Dummy."

"Hey, she would have never let you come, and we need back-up. As much as she hates it, we had to leave her sister and her aunts unprotected. I hated that, and I knew you were nearby anyway," I said.

"You did not," he scoffed.

"I could smell your prissy ass ten miles away," I said.

He put his arm around my shoulder and leaned on me. "I've missed you, Brother."

"I hope you've got more information on all this shit," I said.

"I do, but none of it is good," he said.

"You know I can hear you both, right?" Lyra huffed.

"Damn, Nick. She's perfect!" Sully exclaimed.

"Yes, she is," I muttered.

We entered her small home. I hadn't realized Cort was following us, but he slipped in the door. He made his way around the kitchen like the place was his. Sully and I watched from the living room as he started a pot of coffee and took out four mugs. Lyra disappeared into her bedroom and came back with a smile instead of a scowl. Sully looked confused, as did I.

"Come on in, Aspen," Lyra called out. Lyra's best friend, Aspen LaSalle had pale blonde hair and wide blue eyes. I wondered if she didn't have fairy blood, because of the largeness of her eyes on her delicate face. Cort responded to her entry by placing another mug on the counter.

Aspen sat down on the couch across from Sully and I, looking us up and down. "Which one do I get?" she asked.

"You can have both of them," Lyra said.

"Gay," Sully said, pointing to himself.

"You are still hot," Aspen said.

"True, but you do nothing for me. Cort on the other hand..."

"Straight," Cort said.

"Damn," Sully muttered. I gave him a knowing look, and he shook his head at me. He knew what I was getting at, but he wasn't in the mood.

"I specifically said I didn't want another Alpha in this town. Much less another Faeborn wolf," Lyra reminded me.

"I know what you said, but I also know that I hated leaving your sister and your aunts alone."

"Oh, honey, ain't nothing getting in that house," Aspen said. Cort served her coffee first, then made his way around to the rest of us. I saved that information in the back of my head.

"The wards are strong, but we've seen things that can cross wards," Sully said.

"Like what?" Lyra asked.

"Black wolf," I replied. "One crossed Gloriana's wards in Shady Grove."

"Not just any black wolf. He was a First People's shifter," Sully added.

"There aren't any of those left," Lyra said.

"I know. They killed it," I replied.

"And you let them?" she asked.

"He attacked Grace's son, Callum," I said. "I was there when it happened, but I would have done the same thing. He crossed the wards uninvited with the intent to kill. He had multiple chances to back down, and he didn't. And, he isn't the last of the black wolves. He had children."

"What's special about her son?" Lyra asked.

Sully cleared his throat. I leaned away and looked at him to see if he wanted to answer, but he just blew across his coffee. "Being her adopted son was enough. Grace isn't like other fairies. Her family means everything to her. Even the adopted ones." I wanted to keep Callum's shifted form to myself for now. I might need that secret down the road. I also needed to change the subject.

My brother had a huge crush on Callum Fannon. He had from the moment he saw him, but Callum after the war for Winter took up with a local fairy in Shady Grove. Sully didn't feel comfortable enough around the people there to take a shot at Callum. Plus, at first, he feared Grace. We hadn't had much luck with fairies. Our knowledge of them was that they meddled in wolf affairs and generally fucked things up. I even went to Shady Grove thinking that Grace was the one that was trying to control the packs, but I quickly learned about Grace and how different she was from normal fairies. Sully learned too, but not soon enough to ask Callum out.

"So, I'm supposed to let your brother whom I've never met keep an eye on my family?" Lyra asked.

"No, you can free up some of your own men that you trust to do that. Sully is here to back me up. Plus, he's got information from the other packs in the region," I said.

"How did you end up with two Alphas in one family?" Aspen asked.

"Three actually. My sister, Suzi, has Alpha blood. However, our father and Nick's father were different. Same fairy mother."

"Fucking fairies," Aspen said.

"It's relevant because this coalition of packs was started by our mother," I said. "We've seen how she directs her minions to take over like Rocco Davis and his father, Creed."

"She killed my father who had doted on her for years," Sully said.

"You look to be the same age. Are you?" Aspen asked.

"That's impossible," Lyra said.

"Actually, we are very close in age. I don't know my birthdate because my mother delivered me already born to my father. The best we can tell we are about four months apart in age from one another," I said.

Cort slid onto the couch next to Aspen as Lyra paced the room.

"If he stays, it's on my terms," Lyra said.

"I wouldn't want to do it any other way," Sully replied. "I'm here for my brother, but I am at your mercy as the Alpha of the pack."

"And you are okay with a female Alpha?" she asked.

"Heavens, yes. My sister was going to be a better Alpha than me anyway," Sully replied.

"You were a very good leader," I said. He took a deep breath and thanked me with his eyes. Sully led his pack as his father's heir, leaving his father to do whatever he wanted in Houma, Louisiana. The wolves respected him. Of course, he kept his sexual preferences to himself, but I was willing to bet that every member of that pack didn't give a fuck who he was sleeping with because he took care of his people. Unlike my own father who was weak and allowed our pack to fall. Houma fell, too, but it was due to a direct intervention by our mother. One day, we would make her pay for all the blood on her hands.

"You will not participate in any pack meetings or business. You keep to the sidelines. I don't want you in this fight unless it's to protect his ass," Lyra said, pointing at me.

"It's because she likes my ass," I said to Sully.

"It is a nice ass," Sully replied.

"I think I got it from our mother," I said.

"Me, too," he replied.

"Oh, for heaven's sake!" Lyra exclaimed. Aspen lifted her coffee cup to laugh behind it. Cort bit his bottom lip and looked away.

"I'm sorry. You were saying?" I said, looking up to Lyra innocently. She seethed under the surface, and while I loved her fire, I wanted to see her calm and cool. If she was losing the confidence of her pack, it was because she was losing her temper too much. Animals sense anxiety and fear. She had every right to be afraid of this danger, but she couldn't face it with anger. She needed to face it with confidence. Having allies would help build that confidence. But I'd slept with her, and she didn't trust me. I didn't know how I'd convince her to agree to call for help.

"Stay out of Dog River business," she replied.

"Yes, ma'am," Sully said respectfully.

She muttered to herself, then slumped into a chair across the room. A tired queen on her throne.

"What have you found out?" I asked Sully.

"Several of the packs that have been forced to join the coalition spoke of women wearing red cloaks," he said.

I groaned and leaned back into the couch.

"Red cloaks?" Aspen asked.

"The Order of the Red Cloak was a triad of fairy witches. We killed them all in the war. What? Are these imposters of some sort? Copy-cats?" I asked.

"I don't know, but if the stories are true, they aren't fake. They have real power, and it's dark," Sully said.

"You have a witch friend, right?" I asked Lyra.

"Yes."

I waited for her to expand on her affirmative, but she didn't. Sully grunted behind me, and I wanted to punch him.

"Does she wear a red cloak?" I asked.

"No," Lyra replied.

"Lyra, we talked about this. Help me, help you," I said. Sully let out several grunts and I nudged him. Hard.

"Willow Temperance Luna Peregrine," Aspen said.

"Say that five times," I said to Sully. He rolled his eyes at me. "What kind of witch is she?"

"Wiccan. Pagan. She spends most of her time roaming around the swamp. You can't miss her when she comes to town. Hair is either pink or lavender, and she wears a dress of rags. Occasionally, she carries a staff. She makes small charms and bundles herbs from the forest to sell for money," Aspen said.

"Sounds like a good witch," Sully said.

I wanted to say there was no such thing as a good witch, but a gypsy witch in Shady Grove had changed my opinion about that. However, I still didn't trust ones that I didn't know.

"She is. She's blessed all of our homes and our children," Aspen said.

"You have children?" I asked.

"Our. As in the collective pack, our," she corrected.

"My bad. I'm not used to…"

"…being in a pack," Lyra finished for me. She had relaxed as we talked, and I saw a touch of softness return to her eyes. "Willow isn't a red cloak witch."

"ORC," I said.

"Isn't that trademark infringement or something?" Aspen asked.

"Explain trademarks to the fairy queen, and we will go from there," I said.

"Gotcha," Aspen replied. Cort remained quiet through the whole conversation.

"You know I am going to have to fight him," he said to Lyra.

"No, we aren't doing that," Lyra said.

"The pack will expect it." He was right. If I was going to be passed off as Lyra's match, then Cort's reputation would be damaged by our relationship if he didn't stand up for what was legally his.

"He's right," I said. "I have no desire to fight you, but you are right."

"Everyone will know it's for show," Lyra said.

"We will find a way to do it," I said. "He needs to keep his standing in the pack. He looked pretty fiercesome to me at your aunts' house." I'd remembered Lyra saying he didn't have an Alpha bone in his body, but he was a perfect Beta. I was willing to bet he was one of the few fighters in the pack. Several others had stepped out against Davis, but only when it was clear we had the advantage.

The pack needed to keep their confidence in him. If he lost to me, he kept his dignity because he didn't just allow me to take Lyra. Which made me wonder what she would do after I left. She had no intention of allowing me to stay around her. It didn't matter what her aunts said. I saw the look in her eyes. She wanted me and Sully gone. Mostly me.

SIX

CORT AND ASPEN left after we talked about the members of the pack who were strong enough to fight. We only had about a dozen with a few maybes. In a pack of fifty wolves, I expected more fighters, but the Dog River pack had been established in the early 1700s. In 1732, a Frenchman drew a map of Steelshore Bay. Even then, the Riviere aux Chiens is labelled. The pack came from France to the new world settling in what was once the capital of Louisiana.

The Dog River pack mixed with the various cultures in area including European settlers, Native Americans, and African slaves. Much like New Orleans, Steelshore and its surrounding areas became well known for its mish-mash of culture leaning heavily to the French side of things.

I wondered if Lyra's witch friend used the same dark magic that our former foe, Lisette, used. It was a mix of wild fairy magic and voodoo. A potent combination. However, I'd seen the wreath on Eula and Aggie's door. It didn't seem ominous at all. I didn't think to open my fairy sight and look at it. Levi scolded me quite often about forgetting my fairy side. I didn't think it would help me here with Lyra and the pack, but there were some things that I needed to remember that I could do. Like having a wild card up my sleeve.

"Where is he going to sleep?" Lyra asked.

"I've got a place to stay up the road," Sully replied.

"The Dog River Hotel?" she asked.

"Yes," Sully replied.

"That's a hell hole," she said.

"An actual hell hole or like a dump?" I asked.

She glared at me.

"It's not so bad," Sully said.

"There are already too many people in this house," Lyra said.

"I can't sleep around Nick, anyway. He snores too loudly," Sully said.

"I snore! I think not. You are the snorer. Like sawing logs. Big ones," I teased.

"I'm going to record you the next time you are doing it. I think you dream that it's me when it's actually you," Sully replied.

"Do you do this all the time?" Lyra asked.

"Do what?" we both responded.

"Ugh! Nevermind. I'm starving," she said.

"Well, allow me to take you both out to dinner," I said.

"You wouldn't go out with me when we weren't brothers," Sully said.

"We've never not been brothers. Besides, that didn't stop you," I said, then realized I'd said it out loud.

"Stop him from what?" Lyra asked.

"Nothing," I replied. An evil look glowed in Sully's eyes. "Don't you dare." My warning fell on deaf ears.

"Lyra, I'm sure you will agree with me, even if you don't admit it, that my brother is very handsome. Before we knew of our blood ties, I kissed him to prove a point. A quick, unknown incestuous kiss," Sully said.

"You can stop now," I huffed.

Lyra's eyes widened, and I saw the playful glow in them. "Oh really? Are you bi-, Nick?" she asked.

"No, I am not bi-. I am hetero. This family can only handle one traitorous homo brother," I said.

"He's always been homophobic, too," Sully said, poking his lip out in a ridiculous pout.

"Oh my! How awful for you," Lyra said, offering her hand to Sully. He stood from the couch and took it. He offered her an arm, and she linked her arm through his. I followed them groaning out of the house. The one secret that we shared as brothers, and he went and told it to the woman that I'd attached myself to for better or worse.

"It has been a great burden. Even more so now that he is my brother. I've tried to educate him, but he's so stubborn," Sully went on.

"Stop it," I warned.

Lyra giggled as we made our way back down the street toward Sally's restaurant. "Don't you worry. You are here now, and I have every intention of reforming Dominick Meyer."

"I wish you the best. It will be a long, painful road," Sully said, making Lyra giggle even more.

My brother's charm had won her over. Now, if only I could do the same.

"I think you should stay at the house and make him stay at the hotel," Lyra said.

"No! Absolutely not!" I protested.

They laughed together, and I loved it. Two of my favorite people on this earth, arm in arm, sharing a happy moment at my expense. Suddenly, I was missing Levi who was like a brother to me, too. No. He'd probably join in making me miserable.

The smells of freshly- cooked seafood filled the air as we approached the small restaurant. Lyra waved to one of the waitresses, and we took a seat near the water's edge. A long pier stretched out into the river. The weather was perfect for outdoor eating. Technically, it was late fall, but the coolness in the air indicated that winter was right around the corner.

For once, I was excited about Christmas. I'd be spending it in Shady Grove with my brother, sister, brother-in-law, and my adopted family, the Reardens. But I thought about Landon Crosse today with his bloody face. I might not make it back in time for that dream. My Christmas might be spent here, protecting Dog River. If Lyra cooled her anger, then that might not be such a bad thing, but it wasn't likely that she would calm down until she felt like her pack was safe.

We sat and ate, discussing ways to protect the pack without calling in reinforcements.

"Do you have ties to any of the neighboring packs?" I asked.

"We used to have ties to the Fairhope pack across the bay, but they keep to themselves now. There is a small pack in Bayou La Batre. Maybe 20 wolves. I don't want to drag a smaller pack into this. Maybe they will go unnoticed," Lyra said.

"We might send them a warning. A small pack can disappear easier than a large one," I said.

"Nick, people don't want to leave their homes. I know it's easy for you, because you walked away from yours. The rest of us want to stay and fight," she said. Her words cut deep. It was like she knew my questions about leaving my home and my father. Sully nudged my leg under the table. I looked up to meet his eyes. He wanted me to brush it off, but I think it hurt more because it was Lyra. It was time to dismiss the notion that I was anything other than a means to the end for her.

"I'll run south and warn them tomorrow," Sully said.

"No. I need you here. I'll send Malphas and Echo," I said.

"I thought I saw those two old buzzards," Sully said.

As if on cue, the pair of ravens walked into the restaurant and up to us. I'd had them listening and watching the small town. Neither of them looked like they belonged here. Malphas had a tendency to wear long black trench coats. With his pale skin and dark eyes, he was every goth girl's dream. Echo wore sleek black pants with a white button up shirt. Dark aviator glasses covered his eyes, but his bright smile illuminated his face.

"Lyra, you know Echo and Malphas," I said, introducing them formally.

"More of your friends that I asked you not to call," she said.

"They were already here, plus they are assigned to me by the Queen. They cannot disobey her orders. I'll send them south to warn the other packs. They can even cross the bay to the packs on the other side," I said.

"Good evening, Miss Rochon. We will happily do this business for you with your blessing. We will go in your name, if you so desire. It will spread your name across the packs, building a perception of strength and power," Malphas said with a slight bow. The slick bastard knew exactly what to say to her.

"I would appreciate it. You may go in my name," Lyra responded.

Echo signed and I'd missed the first part so I couldn't

interpret. Malphas did. "My partner says that he's never worked for such a lovely woman."

"Don't tell Grace that," I said.

Echo signed again with Malphas interpreting. "The Queen is a beauty, but I find Lyra to be exotic and exciting."

Lyra blushed and stammered, "Thank you."

Echo grinned widely, and although I couldn't see his eyes, I knew he was taunting me. Bastard.

"Okay. Enough of that. Fly away, Crow," I said, shooing them away.

"Actually, why don't you stay and eat with us?" Lyra said. "I insist."

The two accepted her invitation. We sat and talked about what Malphas and Echo found when they followed Rocco and his minions.

"We followed them all the way across the state-line into Mississippi. They entered a casino in Biloxi. We shifted and followed them, but they went into a back room where we couldn't go," Malphas said.

"I'll call Levi. I'm sure he has someone in his network that can tell us more about the casino. I want to know who owns it," I said. "If you will excuse me for a minute." I stood, leaving them at the table and stepped outside. The sun had almost disappeared, turning the bright town into shadows. A dark feeling swept over me. Suddenly alert, I searched the corners of darkness for the source of the feeling. Magic. Someone was casting a spell. Sully appeared at my side.

"I feel it, too," he said. "It's strong. Like mother's magic."

"Do you think she is here?" I asked.

"We better hope not," he responded. "What did Levi say?"

"I haven't called him, yet."

"Don't let what she said get to you. Now that I've been around her, I realize that she is under a massive amount of stress, and she thinks her feelings for you make her weak. You have to be stronger than her doubts. Stronger than your own."

"Why the hell are you like this?" I asked.

"Am I wrong?" he asked.

"About her feelings, yes. I'm here to help protect her pack. There is nothing else there," I said.

"You are wrong," Sully said.

I shook my head. "Keep an eye out while I call Levi."

Dialing my *other* brother, I waited while the phone rang. I hoped he wasn't in the Otherworld. A familiar voice answered, but it wasn't Levi. "Hello?"

"Callum," I said. Sully spun around to me with his eyes wide. I waved at him, indicating he was supposed to be watching out, not crushing on the Queen's son. "Is Levi around?"

"He's actually not. He and Grace are in the Otherworld. That issue they've been dealing with has gotten bigger," he said.

"Things are never normal, are they?" I said.

He laughed on the other end. "I'll tell him you called. Is there a message?"

"Just let him know I need to find out about a casino in Biloxi. Perhaps he has someone down there that is connected to it. We need to find out who owns it," I said, giving him the name of the casino and its location.

"I'll call you back with the information. You stay safe down there. We are here if you need help," Callum said.

"Thanks, but I've got help," I said.

"Sully is there?" Callum asked.

"Yes," I responded.

"Then, you are in good hands. I'll call back soon," Callum said, disconnecting the call.

"Good news. You are on his radar," I said.

"Would you shut up? He's practically married," Sully said. Callum had been dating Michael Handley since the end of the war for Winter. None of us who knew him thought it was a good match, but he was happy. We felt like we needed to leave it. Of course, when I met Callum I thought he and my brother would get along great, but Callum never showed any interest. Sully hadn't been himself since his father died, and I couldn't blame him for suppressing his normal personality. It hurt to see him that way, but he needed time. He had made progress, but I wasn't sure he was ready yet. One thing was for sure; he liked Callum. Really liked him.

"Yeah, and you aren't interested," I teased. It felt good to prod him instead of him doing it to me.

"Not at all," he said.

We returned to Lyra and the ravens. I told them about the feeling I got, and we decided it was best if we headed home.

Clouds covered the sky, and the dark seemed darker as we walked back to Lyra's house. She spoke to her aunts and decided to leave Tinley there under their protection which meant that Sully could stay. He tried to get out of it, saying I needed to spend some time alone with her, but I assured him that was the exact opposite of what I needed. He reluctantly agreed to sleep on the couch. Lyra thankfully returned to her bed, and I slept in Tinley's room.

No matter what I tried, I couldn't fall asleep. The magic moving in town stayed in the forefront of my mind. We needed magical help. Someone more powerful than me. I could call Rory who was in Steelshore, but I didn't want to take any of Wynnona's team away. Levi and Grace had their hands full. There were others in Shady Grove that would help, but I knew that I had already tested Lyra's trust. Finally, I decided that I only had one other choice. It was time to meet Willow Temperance Luna Peregrine.

SEVEN

TODAY, Willow's hair looked like cotton candy. Pale pink from root to tip. She walked among the leafless trees muttering to herself. Lyra walked next to me. Sully and Tinley walked behind us. Willow stopped at a tall bush which had almost lost almost all of its leaves, except for a few that hung from the branches limply. She took three from the tree which were mostly yellow. She stuffed them in the front of her shirt. Honestly, I didn't think she was wearing a bra, so I wasn't sure where the leaves went.

We followed her through a large thicket of trees to the bank of a stream that lead down to the Dog River. She leaned over it, fishing the leaves from their unknown hiding place. The leaves fell haphazardly into the water and slowly floated away.

Willow squatted down at the bank humming a quiet tune while watching the leaves drift off. I'd heard of Divination, and I wondered if this was a form of it. The edges of her skirt hung into the water, and she began to sway. Once the leaves were gone, she stood up and looked me in the eye. She cocked her head sideways and huffed.

"You aren't what I expected," she said.

"Sorry to disappoint," I replied.

"I'm not disappointed. I just expected someone more wolf," she said.

"Well, I'm half-fairy," I said.

"I know that, but the loss of your hand hinders you," she said, reaching forward. The moment she touched my hand, the magic holding my glamour failed. She stared down at my stump, and I jerked it away from her. "See." She looked at Lyra and shook her head. She began humming again and walked past me and the two behind us.

"What does that mean?" I asked.

"That we are going to lose this fight," Lyra whispered.

"Well, she's wrong. I'm wolf. I'm all wolf. I can prove it," I said in protest. Lyra quirked her lips to the side but said nothing.

"Yeah, yeah. Cool your tits," Sully said.

"Come," Willow called to us. She'd moved further back down the path we'd traveled to get here. We hurried to catch up to her. "It is not an insult, Stumpy. It is just a fact. You have gifts and talents, but you are not what I expected."

"Stumpy?" I asked. Sully giggled like a girl behind me, and I gave him a light fist to the stomach.

"You have a stump, don't you?"

"Well, yes, but I'm doing fine with what I have," I said.

"Really?" she asked, spinning around to face me. "Then stop the glamour. Walk around without the hand."

"Lyra needs strength. Not someone that seems helpless."

"It takes more strength to walk without it than it does

to create the illusion of strength," Willow said.

"I like her," Sully said.

"Shut-up," I responded.

"He's right, Willow. My wolves will think he is broken if he walks around without the glamour," Lyra said.

"And when they find out it's a lie. An illusion of power?" Willow asked. "What will they do then?"

None of us answered her as she continued to walk. She muttered and mumbled until we came to a small log cabin in the woods. She invited us inside with a motion, and we went into the small abode. The walls were lined with herbs. Some were in bundles hanging upside down to dry. Others grew out of small pots and jars.

An honest to goodness cauldron hung over a fire in a stone fireplace. Willow stirred its contents and clapped her hands in glee. She sat down in a rickety chair that I was sure would crumble with her weight, but it didn't.

"Have a seat," she implored us. There were no other chairs. We sat down on the wood planked floor. "I do not judge you harshly, Dominick Conell Meyer. You are a drifter like the leaves in the creek. I watched the pattern of your past in the water. Not your future."

"What did you see?" Lyra asked.

"The leaves spread apart and drifted away," Willow answered as if we knew what that meant.

"I've spent much of my life moving from place to place," I said, hoping to provoke more from her. She had magic, and I could feel it. However, it felt weak compared to the big magic of Grace, Levi, and the others from Shady Grove.

"But you are here now," she said.

"Yes, as long as Lyra needs me," I responded.

"If you push them back once, they will return once you have gone," she said.

"I will stay for as long as it takes," I said. "How long I stay is up to Lyra."

"Sounds like a proposal to me," Sully muttered

"Shut up." Lyra said it this time. Tinley giggled.

"The only way you survive this is if you drop the illusion and be truthful to those around you," Willow said. "None of the leaves stopped along the banks. None got held up by branches. They drifted on to the next horizon." We stared at her for a moment not knowing what else to say. "You may leave now."

"Oh, okay," I said, jumping up from my seat. I offered my glamoured hand to Lyra, but she ignored me, getting up on her own.

We walked through the forest in silence back to Lyra's car. We were on the road back to town for several minutes before Lyra spoke.

"Don't you dare walk around town without your hand," she said. "You know what the wolves will think. And if one of the outsiders sees it, we are doomed."

"I have no intention of walking around without it. The glamour is part of me now. Just like the hand was. Witches and soothesayers rarely tell you exactly what they mean. She had to mean something else," I said.

"She's nuts. Her magic works, but I've never seen her correctly predict anything," Lyra said.

"She predicted that Nick would come," Tinley offered.

"I'm not convinced that Nick is our savior," Lyra said.

"You need to get that stick out of your butt and stop being so mean to him," Tinley said.

"You let the adults handle this," Lyra snapped back.

"Woo! That leaves me out," Sully remarked. Lyra cut her eyes to him in the rearview mirror. I don't know what he did, but a smile formed on her face. It seemed everyone could make her smile, except me.

When we arrived back at Lyra's house, Tinley was pissed. She bolted out of the car and ran into the house. The moment the door closed; she began to scream. We ran inside where we found Rocco sitting alone on Lyra's couch.

"Smells like fairy in here," he said.

I stepped in front of Tinley, nudging her back to Sully who took her out of the house.

"Get out of my house," Lyra said.

"I thought it was his house. You made it out like he was the Alpha. He's a damn drifter. I have sources that say he's been living in an apartment in Steelshore with a little Phoenix," Rocco taunted.

"You better leave her alone," I snarled.

"Oh, I have no desire to tangle with her mother," Rocco said, standing up from the sofa.

"You better worry about Wynonna. She may be small, but she will burn your ass," I said.

He chuckled. "You are funny, Half-breed. It seems my daddy knew you when you were little. We thought you were dead, but looky-loo, here you are. Of course, you are no more Alpha than she is."

The hairs on my arms stood on end, and I suppressed the anger inside of me. "You get the fuck out of this house. If you step into it again or this town, I'll kill you."

"You promised me that last time. You don't keep your promises do you, Nick?" he said.

I launched myself at him, hitting him in his mid-section. The force threw us both into the small sofa. I heard it crack as he rolled over holding me down. My claws extended, and I jammed them into his stomach. He howled but managed to pummel me in the face. A loud growl filled the room as Lyra rushed him. She jumped on his back and buried her fangs into his shoulder.

Swinging around he threw her across the room where

she hit the partition between the kitchen and the living room. The plaster on the wall dented with the force of her body. She slumped to the floor but remained conscious.

I took that moment to unleash a fury of punches on Rocco that had him backing up with his arms in front of his face.

"I'm going to kill you, Rocco," I growled.

His form shifted to full wolf. I swatted the air before I could pull my punch. He jumped over the sofa, crashed through the window, and ran across the lawn as Sully ducked behind the car with Tinley. I wanted to chase him, but Lyra was down.

Running over to her, I knelt down. Blood flowed freely from the splits of skin on my real hand. The other hand never took damage, but it wasn't my dominant hand either.

"Lyra, are you okay?" I asked, gently turning her face to me.

"He was in my house," she whimpered.

"He won't come back," I said. She reached up and wrapped her arms around my neck. A flood of emotion barreled out of her body which shook from the strain. I pulled her close to me as she buried her face into my neck. "Let it out," I coaxed.

I heard Sully behind me. "You okay?"

"Yeah, take Tinley to Eula and Aggie's house," I instructed.

"I'll take care of it," he said. I couldn't see him, but I heard the strain in his voice. He didn't like being in a position where he couldn't fight. I'd been in a few scrapes back at Sully's brewery in Houma, Louisiana. Of course, the brewery closed after his father's death. Sully and Suzi ran for their lives. He'd said that their mother begged them not to leave. She even threatened to make them stay, but they got out. Suzi married Reuben and Sully moved to Shady Grove with me. We shared a mother. She'd rejected me once. I didn't care to find out what she thought of me after that.

Lyra's light sobs stopped, but her body continued to tremble. "I can't do this. They are all going to die because I'm not strong enough."

"I'm here now. We are going to beat them," I said.

"Even Willow sees it. We are doomed," she whispered.

"I refuse to believe that," I said.

"How can you have hope in this situation?" she asked.

"Because a trailer park queen is now the queen of all of Winter. Because a kid from Texas is the King and the most powerful Bard to ever walk the earth. Because a Phoenix gave his power to an adopted human daughter. I could go on and on, Lyra. I believe because I've seen the impossible and unlikely happen. It's going to happen here, too. We just have to weather the storm," I said.

She didn't speak again. We sat on the floor together until she pushed away from me and disappeared into the bathroom. I heard the shower start, so I went into the kitchen to wash the blood off my hands. My werewolf healing ability kicked in to repair the damage to my skin and the bruises that had formed on my chest. I found a broom and swept up as much of the glass as I could inside the living room and outside on the porch.

I sat down on the porch as Sully ran up from down the road. "She's safe in their house."

"Good."

"How's Lyra?"

"She will be fine," I replied.

"Why would he come here alone?" Sully asked.

"I'm trying to figure that out. It doesn't make sense. Maybe he was just testing us. Who knows?"

"You okay?"

"I'm fine," I replied to him. "I'm going to get her to move into the house with her aunts until we can get this window fixed."

"Or we could get Willow to ward it like she did the Aunt's house," Sully suggested.

"And that's another thing. I'm sure Willow meant something else, but I can't figure out what it is. She wasn't talking about my hand." I rubbed my forehead. Sully didn't say anything else but sat down next to me on the porch. His phone dinged, and he looked at it. It was from Suzi. She was checking in on us. He texted her back that we were fine and to stop worrying him. "We need to keep her away from here."

"I know. I told Reuben and Mark to keep an eye on her," he said.

"Mark."

"I heard about him and Winnie. And Winnie and Kyrie," Sully said.

Wynonna Riggs and Mark Maynard, the Alpha of the Shady Grove pack, had been friends since they were children which wasn't so long ago. They were close, and everyone thought that they would end up married. However, Winnie was dating Kyrie Babineau while working in Steelshore. Mark had stayed in Shady Grove to protect his pack as any Alpha should. He'd come to the conclusion that the pack would never accept Winnie as his mate anyway. As a Phoenix, she would only bear one child who would inherit her fiery powers one day. Without a wolf heir, the pack would revolt against Mark. He made the decision to let her go, even though I knew very well that she would always hold a place in his heart. I'd heard recently that he had dated one of the girls from the pack but had broken it off before it ever began. It was going to be harder for him than he thought.

I knew that very well now that Lyra had a piece of me. She may have leaned on me after the fight, but she would never give into me completely. If she only knew that I didn't need for her to submit to me, nor did I want her to do that. We were raised on the old standards of packs where the men controlled the women. I'd seen enough of that in my day to hate the idea of it. My stepmother, Regina, died because she submitted to my father's will. I swore I'd never do that to anyone I cared about.

Also, I needed to admit to myself that part of me wanted to settle down and raise a family. Teach a new generation of wolves to respect their spouses, to accept those who are different, and to reach out to the pack to help. The glass I'd swept up sat in the dustpan, and I thought back to all the things that had been destroyed in Shady Grove, but it was always rebuilt. The community would come together and embrace those who had lost and rebuild. I was sure the pack knew that Lyra had been attacked. They should be here fixing the damn window and providing support, but they weren't.

"Where is the pack?" I voiced my thoughts.

"I'm not sure. Most of them hang out at that dive bar across from Sally's," Sully said.

"Let's go have a chat with them," I said.

"Oh, shit. Are you really going to stir this pot?" he asked.

"Are you with me or not?" I asked.

"I'm hurt that you even had to ask," he replied. I knew that he was. I knew that he always would be. But more than anything, I wanted my brother to find his happy ending.

EIGHT

SULLY and I marched into the Dive Bar like we owned the joint. Some of the patrons murmured as we entered, but most went on about drinking their beers and playing pool. I grabbed a large glass mug from a guy sitting closest to where I stood. Raising in the air, I slammed it down on the table breaking the glass and the table. The man and his friend jumped up from their seats.

"What the fuck?" he yelled.

"I was told there was a wolfpack in this town. Was I misinformed?" I asked over the crowd. I'd garnered their attention. "Well, are there wolves here or not?"

One man in particular flashed his eyes and fangs at me. I crossed the room to him, lifting him out of his chair by the collar.

"Let go of me, asshole!" he yelled.

I let him go by throwing him across the room into a group of guys next to the pool table. Looking over my shoulder, I watched my helpful brother lean against the wall. He gave me a nod.

"If you're wolves, then I'm ashamed of you," I said.

"You need to watch your words, Wanderer," a man holding a cue stick said.

"Why is that, Coward?" I asked.

"We aren't cowards," he snapped back.

"Prove it!" I dared. I knew I'd regret this, but it needed to be done.

He rushed me along with two others including the one I'd thrown at the pool players. I dodged one, then dropped into a crouch to swipe the second's legs out from under him. The cue stick guy swung the rod at me, I grabbed it, growled, and snapped it into pieces. He took several swings at me, but I put him down quickly.

"Who's next?" I yelled.

None of them would look me in the eye. They were cowards. The whole lot of them. "Your Alpha was attacked in her own home today, and you're sitting here sipping beer like it's a fucking holiday. You should be down at her house, fixing the window or the furniture. You could help protect her sister or her aunts. But instead, you sit on your hairy asses like yellow bellied muskrats. I took three of you out like it was child's play. You're a disgrace. I'm disgusted that any of you dare to call yourself a wolf."

"Big words for a half-breed," the bartender said.

"They are the words of a wolf. They are the words of a man who has seen a lot of shit, and I know strength. There is no power here," I said.

"Would you like a drink?" he asked.

"No, thanks. I've got a window to fix," I said.

The bartender leaned over the stained wooden bar, flashed his eyes at me, and grinned. "You gonna pay for your mess?"

"Sure. Put it on my tab," I said. Sully walked over to

him and slapped several hundred-dollar bills on the counter.

"I pay his tab," Sully said.

"You're right, Son," the bartender said, folding the money and pocketing it. "Bar's closed. Get the fuck out!"

The people grumbled but exited as he instructed. I waited to leave to thank him. "I appreciate it," I said after the last one left.

"Be careful that you don't start a fire that you can't handle," he said.

"What's your name, Sir?" I asked.

"Hector," he replied.

"Thank you," I said then looked at him through my sight which I rarely used. A blue aura swirled around him. "You are fairy."

"And?" he asked.

"What kind?" I asked.

"Does it matter?"

"Well, I once knew a bartender who was a lot like you," I responded.

"Kelpie," he replied.

"I knew it," I said with a smile. "I'll bring them back to drink if they show up to help."

"They will, but you gotta give them time," he said. "Ignorance is deeply rooted in the core of people, and awareness takes time."

"We don't have time," I responded, then left the bar with Sully in tow.

Lyra stood on her porch speaking to two of the men I'd seen in the bar. I ran up ready to explain my actions when she looked at them then at me. I didn't see anger. However, she was confused.

"What are they talking about?" she asked.

"I don't know. I just got here," I said.

"They say that you helped them to see that they should be here helping me fix the window," she said.

"Yeah, packs do that. They help each other. Support their Alpha," I said with a nod to the two men.

"Guys, this is Dominick Meyer. He's come to help us with the outsider problems. Nick, this is Wade Smithauser and Albert Handman," Lyra said. "I don't think I need your help. Thank you though."

"Hold up a minute. May I talk to you alone for a minute?" I asked.

She rolled her eyes at me and stepped back into the house. I followed her while Sully struck up a conversation with Al and Wade.

"What is it?" she asked.

"It's not about whether you need their help or not. Your pack is suffering from a lack of community. It's not your leadership that's the problem. It's that none of them have a desire to do anything for their fellow wolves besides buy them a round at the bar," I said.

"So, you want me to let them help so they can be good neighbors?" she asked.

"Is that so hard to comprehend?" I asked. Wrong phrasing. Very, very bad phrasing.

"I may not be some high-browed Winter knight, but you don't have to condescend to me, Nick Meyer!"

"You're right. That came out completely wrong," I said.

She growled and stomped out of the house. I put my hands on my hips and listened to her tell the guys that they could help. They were going to go back to their homes and grab some tools. Sully came in the house.

"How does paw taste?" he asked.

"Shut-up," I said.

"I've seen you with other women. You've always been a smooth operator. Why can't you do that with her?" he asked.

"She sees through all of it. I can't separate just helping her and wanting her," I said.

"Well, at least you admit how you feel about her."

"It doesn't matter. She's not having it."

"I guarantee that if you stay the course, she will be very thankful when it's over," he said. "Wow. You broke the sofa."

"Rocco."

"We still haven't figured out why he was here," Sully said as Lyra walked in the door. When she looked at me, it was like I couldn't breathe. I needed fresh air. I needed to get Sully's voice out of my head

"I'm going for a run," I said.

"A run?" she asked.

"Yes, my beast needs to breathe," I said, pushing past her. "Sully, if Malphas shows back up, ask him to go get my motorcycle in Steelshore."

"Sure," Sully replied.

I heard him tell her that she should give me some space to figure things out. Running to the nearest tree line, I sprinted into the woods. When I felt like I'd cleared civilization, I shifted into my wolf form and dashed through the forest. The smells of the nearby swamp filled the air, but the pines overshadowed the murky feeling.

My mind raced through all the questions and variables. It also came back to Willow's words again and again. "Drop the illusion and be truthful." It resonated with me, but I couldn't figure out what illusion she meant.

Finally, I felt fatigued and shifted back to human,

clothing myself with my Winter magic. I sat down on a large stone overlooking the swamp.

"It's not every day that I meet a Faeborn wolf," a deep voice said.

I jumped up from the stone and moved away from the water which began to shift and swirl. A giant alligator slowly moved onto the bank, and I looked behind me to see if I had room to run. His massive jaws housed sharp teeth, and I was more than a little afraid. My father had taught me that a gator could swallow a child, and that I should avoid them as a human, but never go near them as a wolf.

His jaw moved slightly as he chuckled.

"Did you just laugh?" I asked the beast.

He rose up on two legs, towering above me. I was frozen looking at his height and his power. He shifted before my eyes to a man with dark skin and a large toothy grin.

"I'm Henri," he said, offering me a slightly clawed hand.

I shook his hand, because this was not a man I wanted to offend. "I'm Nick."

"Nice to meet you, Nick. What brings you to Dog River?" he asked.

"I'm here to help the pack," I said.

"Ah! I've heard that Lyra Rochon has had some trouble establishing her rule. Her aunts are nice ladies and I'm sure she will figure it out. I smell her on you," he said, still grinning.

"We, uh, are, well, we were involved, but not anymore," I said, not realizing that it was inappropriate for me to talk about her with a stranger. But his massive size and his long fingernails distracted me. "I didn't know there were alligator shifters."

His chest rumbled with another low laugh. "Nick, there are all sorts of shifters. Birds, wolves, bears, deer. I've even seen a possum shifter."

"Hey, me too. He has an armadillo girlfriend," I said.

"So, why not gators?" Henri asked.

"Why not?" I echoed. "I'm here to help Lyra because some outside wolves are trying to move into the territory. My brother and I are going to try to get her wolves to step up in the fight."

"Or you will fight them yourself?"

"If need be."

"This is not a fight you will win alone." After my ruckus in the bar, I was feeling pretty confident. However, Henri burst my bubble. "You are strong, but packs are stronger. Her pack isn't cohesive, and I doubt that even you could turn it around for them."

"I have to try," I said.

"A wise man once said, 'Do or do not. There is no try'."

"Did you just quote Star Wars to me?" I asked.

"Yoda is wise."

"But hardly a man!"

"Man. Green alien. Green gator. Same difference." He sat down on the rock that I had once occupied. Four alligators rose to the surface, watching me closely. "Part of my pack. They won't harm you."

"I'll stand over here just the same."

"You offend me." One of the gators snapped his jaws, and I scurried over to sit next to Henri on the rock. "That's better. I have something to tell you."

"Wait! Your pack. You're the Alpha?"

"I am the King."

"Oh, okay. Nice. You have something to tell me?"

"Yes. It was two weeks ago when one of my men came to me telling me about a witch moving through the swamp on a magical cloud of mist. I followed him to the spot where he saw her, but we could not track her. We are poor trackers above water. However, one week ago, I got the same report, and I saw the witch."

"Pinky-purple hair?" I asked, thinking he'd seen Willow.

"I know Willow. This was not her."

"Oh."

"This witch had black hair and pale skin. She wore a red cloak."

"Shit," I muttered.

"You know these witches?"

"I thought we killed the ORCs."

"ORCs?"

"Order of the Red Cloak. We killed them in the war for Winter."

"Then you know the Queen?"

"I do. Her husband is like a brother to me. You said witches?"

His eyes darkened. "Yes. The one we followed met up with two others. They were conducting a spell. I don't claim to know about those things, but we cleared out. Darkness followed them, and I wanted my people away from them."

This was bigger than me or Lyra. We needed help, but I refused to call without speaking to Lyra first. I didn't know how I would convey to her how dangerous the situation was if the ORCs were involved.

"I need to go back. How can I repay you, Henri?"

"No need, Son. If you can get rid of them, I'd appreciate it though. If not, we will move to a different swamp."

I shook his hand again, then sprinted back following my own scent back to Lyra's house. Emerging from the woods, I saw Sully dragging Lyra out of the house as she yelled at two men who were working on the broken window.

As I ran toward them, Sully yelled at me. "Run!"

A blur of white fur hit me on my side, knocking me to the ground. I looked up at Sully and Lyra who hit the ground as the house exploded.

NINE

MY EARS RANG as I regained consciousness. Lyra stood over me, patting my face. "Nick! Wake up! Wake up!" she screamed.

"What happened?" I asked.

"Bomb. There was a bomb in the house," she said.

"A white wolf. There was a white wolf," I said.

"It ran. It was the ghost wolf," she said. "It's been haunting me."

"What?" I said, looking at the smoldering debris. A fire engine approached, and I looked back up at Lyra. "Where's Sully?"

"He's fine. He's looking for Al and Wade," she said. "I don't think they got out of the way." Tears formed in the corners of her eyes, and my testosterone kicked in. I pushed off the ground with a groan and helped her up as the police and firefighters arrived.

"Are they humans?" I asked.

"Some, but we have people in the departments. They will cover up any wolf activity."

"A bomb will bring out the human authorities," I said. "That's why Rocco was there."

"To plant the bomb."

"Yes, and to get us distracted with the investigation."

"Do we tell them that he was here?" she asked. Normally, we kept these types of things to ourselves which Rocco had bet on. But in this case, having the cops chasing him might help us.

"Tell them he was here. Tell them that he stays in the casino in Biloxi." She nodded as we walked up to the firefighters. One of them approached us.

"Hey, Lyra," he said.

"Nick, this is James McCaffrey. He's one of mine," she said. "I mean. One of the wolves. Not mine."

"I'm pretty sure I was yours once or twice," he said with a smile. He offered me his hand, but like the immature wolf who decided to be territorial at the worst moment, I didn't take it. Lyra growled but I ignored her. "Ah! I see. Sorry. It was a long time ago."

"There was a bomb in my house. Two of the guys were here helping me fix my window. Our friend Sully is looking for them," she said.

Sully ran up to us, which meant he heard her say his name. His hearing was always better than mine. "I found them."

"Are they okay?" she asked. He shook his head. "No? They are dead?"

"The blast was strong," Sully said.

She turned to me with her nostrils flaring. "You encouraged them to come to my house. You brought them to this danger." She shoved me. "Their blood is on your hands."

"Lyra, I..." I tried to protest, but she kept shoving me.

Sully moved toward us, but I put my hand up to tell him to stay out of it.

"You are not helping, Nick! You are making it worse. This pack is not like your ideal utopia of Shady Grove. We have real dangers here. Two of my guys are dead, and now I've got to tell their wives and their children that their father isn't coming home!" she screamed.

"Lyra, it's okay. It's no one's fault," James said, stepping between us. She snarled at him, but he didn't back down.

"Lyra!" Tinley's frantic voice cut through the noise. "Lyra!"

Lyra stared at me as her sister yelled for her. "Leave, Nick. Don't come back." She ran around James to Tinley. The sisters embraced.

"She will calm down. She always does," James said.

"Yeah," I replied.

"We should do as she asks for now," Sully said. "I've got a room at the hotel. Come on."

"But I should stay here with her even if she…"

"Nick, she asked you to leave."

My heart sank as I accepted her decision. Sully hung his arm around my shoulders as we began to walk away. "We aren't leaving town. Just leaving her to be with her family right now."

"It feels wrong," I said.

"You can't help someone who doesn't want to be helped," he said.

We trudged three miles to the tiny hotel. I slipped into the bathroom as soon as we arrived. I needed a shower and time to think. The lukewarm water poured over me as I stood under it. I needed to know what Levi found out about the casino. Malphas and Echo would be back soon, and we could discuss our next move. If worst came to worst, I would call in reinforcements. We would deal with the issue outside of Dog River Territory. I'd still do whatever I could to protect her, even if she didn't think she needed protecting. There was a time when I thought the same thing. Sully and Suzi saved me. I don't even remember what the turning point was. Things changed, and my heart changed.

I got out and found clean clothes waiting for me on the counter. Sully and I were about the same size, but he wore nicer clothes than I did.

When I stepped out of the bathroom, Sully sat on one of the beds while texting on his phone. The glow of the device illuminated his face. I saw the similar features in our faces that I had dismissed when we first met.

"Feel better?" he asked.

Ignoring his question, I said, "I met the King of the Alligators today."

"What the wha?"

"Henri Beaufort. Extremely nice, but fearsome fellow. He told me that he's seen three red cloaked witches in the swamps," I said.

"New ones?"

"Seems so. I need to call Levi. We have got to know about the casino, and he and Grace need to know about the witches. I'm out of my league with them," I said.

"You are not. How many times has she gotten on to you about dismissing your fairy side? It's very strong. They've both felt it."

"Yours is, too."

"Then we can handle the witches."

"You don't know a lick of magic," I said.

"You can teach me."

"I don't know much more than a lick."

"Please stop talking about licks. It's been too long," Sully groaned.

"Maybe you should have told him you were interested," I said.

"Maybe you should let that go," he replied.

"Did you see the white wolf at Lyra's? The one that tackled me?"

"I saw it."

"Is he here?" I asked.

"That wasn't Callum," he said.

"Are you sure?" I asked, skeptically.

"Trust me. I know Callum. That wasn't him."

I didn't press him, but I wondered. "Then there is another white wolf."

"When I talked to some of the townsfolk, they told me about a white wolf. They called it a ghost wolf. I thought it was just superstition, but maybe there is something to it. The wolf saved you," Sully said.

"I'm calling Callum," I said which I knew would get a rise out of him.

"Why! Don't bring him into this!" Sully said. I grinned at him being protective of a man he wasn't interested in.

"Callum can hold his own, but I'm just going to ask about the Native American white wolves," I said. I immediately called Callum's number, but he didn't answer. I called Hot Tin Roof Bar where he worked.

"Hot Tin Roof!" a man answered.

"Hey, this is Nick," I said.

"I know who you are," the man said.

"Oh, okay. I'm looking for Callum."

"He's not here. You don't know who this is do you?" the man taunted.

"I'm sorry. I don't," I replied.

"It's Killian," he said.

Killian was Grace's youngest son. This person sounded like a full-grown man. We'd seen Killian just a week or so ago, and he was still a teenager.

"I just saw Killian last week. Now who is this?" I asked.

"You are funny, Uncle Nick. Everyone teases me because I sound older on the phone," Killian said. "Oh, Dad is here. Want to talk to him?"

"Yes, please," I replied, trying to shake off the idea that Killian would be matured enough to fight with us soon.

"Hello," Levi answered.

"What are you feeding that kid?" I asked.

"He eats like a horse, but he's still a teen. His voice changed a couple of days ago. It's disturbing to say the least," Levi said. "I guess you are calling about the casino."

"Well, I need to talk to Callum, but yes, I need that info, too."

"Where are you?" he asked.

"Dog River Hotel," I replied.

"Okay. Move out of the center of the room," he replied. The phone clicked off, and a huge glowing portal opened. Levi Rearden, King of Winter, stepped through with his sword, Excalibur. "We need to talk face to face."

"Okay then," I said.

"Oh, hey, Sully," Levi said.

"Your majesty," Sully said, lowering his head.

"Oh, shit. Quit that. I get enough of that in fairy. Not interested in my friends doing it. Especially not in private," Levi said.

"What do you have for me?" I asked.

"You aren't going to like it."

TEN

LEVI PRODUCED a file out of thin air. Damn fairy magic. He slapped it down on the bed, and we gathered around it. Picking it up, I flipped through the contents. It mapped out how many casinos were owned by the same company. One in Biloxi, one in New Orleans, one in Atlantic City, and two in Las Vegas. I took a deep breath when my eyes landed on the name of the owner.

Araxia Meyers Holdings, Incorporated.

"That bitch is using my father's name," I growled.

"I told you that you weren't going to like it. Tennyson's old network has a few insiders in each of the casinos. I've sent word that I need visual confirmation of the owners and managers of the facilities. I'm waiting on that info now. As soon as I get it, you will have it," Levi said.

Sully placed his hand on my shoulder to calm me. "Are we sure it is our mother?" he asked Levi.

"That's why I want photos. We need to be sure," Levi replied.

"There is something else," I said, gathering my wits.

"What's that?" Levi asked.

"I met the Alligator King yesterday. He says there are three red cloaked witches in the swamps conducting rituals and spells," I said.

Levi stepped back and shook his head. "We eliminated the Order of the Red Cloak."

"I said the same thing. It's either imposters or we are in deep shit," I said. "I believe that one of them is Araxia or Celinette or whatever the fuck her name is." Talking about my mother always made me angry. She'd tossed me to my father like I was trash, but she had married Sully's father and seemed to be a good mother until the day she murdered her husband.

"The situation in the Otherworld is getting tense or I'd stay here to help. You know you can call Winnie, Mark, or any of our people to help," he said.

"No, I can't. Lyra forbid it." Sully started shaking his head to Levi, but it didn't stop the bard from asking.

"Woman problems?"

"Oh, you know. Her house exploded. Two people died, and she told me to go to hell." Levi started chuckling, and Sully tried not to join him. "It's not funny. Two good guys died."

"I'm not laughing about their deaths." He put his hand on my shoulder. "I'm laughing because you found your Grace."

"Yeah, well, Grace can be a bitch sometimes."

"I should punch you for talking about my wife like that, but I happen to agree with you. And, as you know, it's something she's very proud of."

"Yeah, so how did you finally get her?" I asked, knowing the answer.

"I was patient. She came to me."

"We might not have that kind of time," I said.

"Love always finds a way. That goes for you, too," Levi said to Sully. Levi was Callum's surrogate dad, and I got the impression that he knew about my brother's attraction to the white wolf.

"Yeah," Sully mumbled.

"You are a sorry pair. Pick your balls up and get back out there. Fix this. Don't make me come back down here," he said, pulling his sword out of thin air. It glowed with Winter blue fairy power. "Home." Just like that, he disappeared.

Sully grabbed his crotch. "What are you doing?" I asked.

"I'm pretty sure I've still got my balls," he said. "Do you?"

I sighed. "Barely."

After two days of searching the swamps, Sully, Malphas, Echo, and I hadn't found any sign of the four witches. Levi had texted us pictures of the owner of the casino in Biloxi. There was no mistaking our mother. She was right there across the state line conducting this attack on Lyra's people.

We were standing in Sully's room at the hotel waiting for him to finish primping. "Would you hurry up? We are going to be late."

He stepped out of the bathroom in a sleek black suit with a white shirt. Crisp and clean. He looked great. I pulled at my collar wishing I hadn't worn a tie, but it was a funeral. I hoped that Lyra wouldn't make a scene. I wanted to pay my respects to the dead, but if my presence caused a problem, I'd leave.

"How do I look?"

"Like an overdone fairy," Malphas said. He wore his black on black ensemble, whereas Echo had gone with navy.

"Perfect," Sully responded.

Malphas had driven my motorcycle from Steelshore, and Echo had driven one of the SUVs owned by the F.B.I. (The Fairy Bureau of Immigration was established by the crown of Winter. Currently, Wynonna Riggs was heading it up in Steelshore during my absence.) We piled into the SUV, then drove to the cemetery to find a small gathering at two graves.

When I stepped out of the vehicle, I had to hold in my anger. James McCaffrey stood next to Lyra with his arm around her. She didn't turn to look at us, which was probably for the best. We approached the gathering quietly and stood in the back row. Tinley turned around and saw us. The minister was reading a passage from a book, but Tinley bolted out of her chair and ran to me. I caught her as she threw herself into my arms. I felt her body shake with tears.

"Hey, it's okay," I said.

"She told me that she made you leave," she whispered.

"No. I'm still here. Just backing off for a while until she needs my help," I whispered back.

"She needs you now even if she doesn't admit it."

"That's the thing. I can't make her. I won't."

"I know," she said, hugging me tighter. I let her. She needed it. Sully rubbed her back, and she gave him a small smile. When I lifted my eyes from Tinley, I saw the Alpha flash in Lyra's eyes. Thankfully, she remained in her spot. I knew as soon as it was over that we needed to go. But I didn't want to let go of Tinley. She was afraid, and she didn't trust Lyra to take care of her.

The service ended. Many of the wolves greeted me

which surprised me. When the crowd cleared, I stood with Tinley hugging my side. Malphas and Echo moved closer to the vehicle, while Sully stood at my side.

Lyra approached, but her march was cut off by two old women.

"Well, Alpha boy, we thought you were gone," Eula said.

"It's good to see you," Aggie added.

"I'm sorry it was at such an occasion," I replied.

Lyra started to speak, but Eula cut her off. "Why don't you come to our house? We are having dinner. You and your brother should come."

"I'm not sure that's a good idea," I replied.

"Oh, please, Nick. Please come," Tinley begged.

"I will only come with the permission of the Alpha of Dog River," I said, looking to Lyra.

"Please, Lyra," Tinley continued.

Lyra seethed. She was outnumbered and I'd put the decision on her. If she said no, I would make sure that Tinley understood that it wasn't about her. If she said yes, I might still decline the offer.

Who was I kidding?

"I will not stand in your way even though I told you to leave," Lyra said. "I won't be coming to dinner. I have plans with James."

"Lyra!" Eula scolded.

"It's true. He's waiting on me in the car. You enjoy dinner." She walked closer to me. "If you think I didn't know you are held up in that backward hotel, then you are sorely mistaken."

"As the Alpha of the pack here, I would assume that you knew everything in your town," I replied.

"I *let* you stay here," she said.

"Yes, you did. Why is that?" I asked.

"Because my sister likes you," she replied, then walked between Sully and I to James who waited for her outside his car.

"That went well," I smirked.

"She will come around," Aggie said.

"Not so sure about that. I hear McCaffrey is a good man," I said. I'd asked around about him and several of the people in town that would talk to me said that McCaffrey was well respected in the community. His father had been Lyra's father's Beta.

"He is, but he's not an Alpha. She received word yesterday that the men would be coming back in three days with our new Alpha. She's worried," Eula explained.

After talking to Henri and Levi, she had every right to be worried. We all needed to be very concerned about who was going to show up as the new Alpha. My bets were on Creed Davis even though I knew he had no Alpha blood in him. Unless Araxia had found a way to make an Alpha, then it wasn't Creed. Of course, she had made Suzi, Sully, and me. She probably had several Alpha children.

The full moon would rise in three days. Werewolves were at their peak of power during a full moon. We were tough all of the time, but the full moon enhanced our abilities. I'd never understood why the full moon, but I figured if the moon could control the tides, then it could affect our power.

"Did someone say lunch?" Sully asked.

"Meet us at the house," Aggie said.

We helped the ladies to their Lincoln Town Car which Tinley was driving for them. Sully and I were left alone in the cemetery with the ravens. Malphas and Echo decided to fly and take a look around while we were having dinner.

On the way to the matriarchs' house, I stewed thinking about Lyra and James. Sully noticed.

"I'm proud of you for not ripping out his throat. I mean, I totally would have," he said.

"Yeah, that's why Michael Handley still breathes?"

"That's not funny. I was trying to be funny and you went and ruined it," he huffed, crossing his arms over his chest like a child.

"I'm sorry. I don't even want to know what she is doing with him. What they have done. None of it."

"Heartbreak sucks," he said.

"Was there ever anyone in Houma that you were attached to?" He'd kept his sexual orientation a secret to protect his hold on the Alpha heir. I'd never seen him with anyone in particular, but he would disappear from time to time. I'd never asked him about it, because I figured if he wanted to talk about it, then he would.

"Yeah, for a little while," he said. "But it didn't work out."

"Why?"

"He wanted more, and I refused him," Sully said.

"You were trying to keep your relationship a secret," I surmised.

"No. If I had loved him, then I would have done anything for us. I didn't love him. I liked him a lot, and we had a good time together. However, I never bonded with him like you are with Lyra. That tether that ties you together, it never happened for us," he said.

"Do you feel that pull with Callum?" I asked.

"Callum doesn't know I exist."

"Actually, he does. He asked about you when I talked to him," I said. "Plus, that didn't answer my question."

"I am drawn to him, but I don't know for sure. It's not some magical destiny sort of thing. Look at Grace and Dylan and Levi."

I knew Grace's story very well. I was there the night

Dylan died. I was also there when she finally gave into Levi. She loved them both. If there was a such thing as destiny, hers led her to both of them.

"Destiny or not, I'm challenging you to step up. If you are interested, stop making excuses and ask him. What's the worst he could say? No? You've been rejected before, right?" I asked.

"I have, but I'm so tenderhearted," Sully said poking out his bottom lip.

I snorted at him. "Besides. Whatever it is going on with Lyra and I only makes her more and more mad. Now it's pushed her to James McFiery. It's been doomed from the beginning. I need to find another wolf."

"Have you seen Mark's sisters lately?" Sully asked.

"Ew! No, they are kids," I said.

"They are very adult-looking teenagers," he said. He was trying to get me riled up. Not proposing I become a pedophile.

"There are plenty of wolves in the forest," I joked, as we pulled into the gravel drive at the yellow clapboard house. We didn't mention it again until the aunts brought it up. However, just before we were welcomed inside by Tinley, he had to ask. I had wondered how long he would hold it. Not as long as I expected.

"So, Callum asked about me?"

ELEVEN

EULA AND AGGIE were amazing women. They'd prepared the meal before the funeral with Tinley's help. They entertained us as if we were close family. Their interaction mesmerized me. So much wisdom and knowledge filled their every word. I'd formed an appreciation for them, but now, I truly saw their worth as leaders in the community. It was more than their age, but an understanding of each other, thus understanding human and wolf interactions. As sisters, they were very different in their views, but their combined understanding of life seemed like a joined path in the woods.

The old adage of taking the path less travelled seemed to have culminated in rejoining those paths as they came back to the pack.

"You worked on airplanes for the United States Air Force?" Sully asked in fascination.

"That I did," Eula replied. "Back then, everyone, not just the men, chipped in to help the war effort." She was a regular Rosie the Riveter.

"Tell them what you were doing, Aunt Aggie," Tinley prodded.

"Hush, Child," she responded.

"What were you doing?" Sully pressed.

"I was a dancer in a cabaret show in Steelshore. I lived here, but spent most of my time up river," she said.

"Savoy Palace?" I asked.

"You naughty boy," Eula scolded.

I blushed even though I'd not been in Savoy in a very long time. "I work in Steelshore," I muttered. Sully tried to cover his laugh beside me. I nudged him which made him laugh harder.

"Ah, yes, I suppose keeping an eye on Scarlett O'Lear is in your best interest. She is the reason why I left the Savoy," Aggie said.

"What did she do?" I asked, knowing that Scarlett was on our prime suspect list for the fairy trade.

"A story for another time," Aggie replied. "Lyra tells me that you went to see Willow."

"Yes. I'm sure she told us something important, but for the life of me, I can't figure out what it was," I said.

"She can be vague, and she does it on purpose. She could tell you the answer, but that defeats the point of the journey," Eula said.

Eula and Aggie worked in tandem telling us stories about Willow who was much older than she looked to us. I didn't think she was older than thirty, but age is deceiving in our world with glamours and magic.

"Did you see a feu follet?" Aggie asked.

"A what?" I'd never heard of such a thing.

"Ah, I thought you would know that one considering you grew up in the swamps. The feu follet of the swamps is a ghostly light that will lead you astray or so they say. Some call them will o' wisp or pixie lights," Eula said.

"Some say they are the souls of the fairy dead who are trapped here instead of passing through the tree. Some say they are cursed souls who are omens of death," Aggie continued.

"There are those in Louisiana who believe them to be vampiric and they suck the blood of the children that they lead into the swamps at night," Eula said.

"I saw one once," Tinley interrupted.

Aggie and Eula grabbed for the saltshaker. Eula won, tossing a bit over her left shoulder, then handed it to Aggie. "It's too late, Sister. The devil already has you," Aggie said, tossing a bit over the left shoulder.

"We cannot tell all of our secrets in one night," Eula replied.

"Where did you see it?" I asked Tinley.

"In the woods," she replied.

"When was this?!" Aggie demanded. Tinley curled inside herself, hiding away from the attention she'd drawn to herself.

"Answer," Eula urged.

"A week before Nick arrived. I was walking along the edge of the woods, and I saw it in the trees near the swamp," Tinley explained. Her bravery grew, and she continued to describe it. "A bright blue light like a sparkling sapphire illuminated a small path. I stepped toward it to get a better look, but it moved away. Each time I stepped, it moved. Then, I realized what it was and ran back to safety."

Eula and Aggie muttered to each other. "Perhaps we should end our evening of fun. Thank you, Nick for bringing your brother to dinner. You are welcome to join us at any time," Eula said.

"We would love to have you back," Aggie added.

Tinley crawled back into her cocoon, hiding her face

from us. I'd felt the sudden shift in mood, but I didn't dare question it.

"Well, thank you for a wonderful dinner. I'll definitely come back just to hear some of your stories. I bet you have tons," I said, standing up from my chair. Sully stood next to me. "Tinley, are you okay?" I didn't want to be too bold, but I didn't like to see her frightened.

"I'm okay," she said. "Thank you for coming." She didn't lift her head to look at me. I wanted to circle the table and make her. I needed to know she was alright. However, I let it go. I knew she was safe in this house.

"Goodnight, Ladies. We will see ourselves out," I said. Sully and I left the women. We heard them murmuring as we went out the door.

"What the hell just happened there?" Sully asked.

"I'm not sure," I replied. "I'm worried about Tinley. Lyra says that she doesn't shift. She's too old to not shift."

Sully patted me on the shoulder. "She's okay. I think she's stronger than she looks."

"I hope so. I wish Lyra would let me take her to Shady Grove. She would be protected against whatever is coming," I said, as we walked down the sidewalk to our car.

A whooshing noise made me spin around with my fists up to find Malphas in his goth gear standing behind me. A few black feathers floated in the air.

"I can show you what is coming," he said.

"How?" I asked.

"The Alpha that is coming here will be in a small city just across the state line called Orange Grove. We found several places to hide and observe, but we'd need to leave now to make sure we are in place for his arrival," Malphas said.

"Where is Echo?"

"Keeping an eye on things there. He's fine," Malphas replied. I knew the pair had a supernatural connection.

"We should change clothes," I said.

"You will need to hurry," Malphas replied. I wasn't sure what his urgency was, but I knew he wouldn't lie to me.

Just before we got into the SUV, a car pulled up to the curb, and Lyra climbed out of the passenger seat. She looked angry. Of course, lately, all she had was a resting bitch face. She spoke to the man in the car. I assumed it was James, so like the bad wolf that I was, I used my keen sense of hearing to eavesdrop.

"I'll see you tomorrow," she said.

"Lyra, I don't want to do this."

"I'm your Alpha, and I'm telling you that you have to do it," she urged. She sounded desperate.

"It's not right," he replied. "Please don't force me to do it."

"It's for the best," she replied.

"You know I'd do anything for you," he said.

"Then what is the problem here?" she asked.

"I just wanted to make sure you knew that I disagreed with the decision," he said. "Be safe, and I'll see you tomorrow."

She backed away from the vehicle, and he pulled away. Nothing in the conversation sounded remotely romantic, which confirmed that she was using her ex to piss me off. She'd have to try harder.

"I know you heard that," she said, standing about ten feet from us. "How was dinner?"

"Eula and Aggie are a delight. I enjoyed it immensely," I said.

"Me too," Sully chimed in.

I saw the whites of her eyes as she rolled them. "It's none of your business."

"Gotcha," I replied. She hesitated, then walked toward the front door.

Just before she went inside, she took a last look at us.

"You should tell her," Sully mumbled.

"She has wolf hearing," I muttered back.

"Tell me what?" she demanded. She needed an excuse to get closer to me, and she'd found it. Or rather, my brother served it up to her on a silver platter.

"Malphas found out some information. We are going to check it out. Might be out of town tomorrow," I said.

"I ordered you to leave anyway," she said.

Suddenly, I wasn't in the mood to placate her. I took two steps toward her and looking down into her eyes. "Let's get one thing straight, Lyra. You asked me to come and help. I will not leave this town, you, or Tinley until I know for certain that you are safe. You can pull your Alpha shit on me all you want, but you and I both know that you don't want me to leave."

"That's not true," she said, shifting her weight back on her heels.

I took another step which invaded her personal space. Her hand jerked up to my chest to press me away. However, her effort was weak at best.

"I mean it. None of us are leaving. I made a promise, and I intend to keep it. Whether you like it or not is entirely up to you, but I'd like to see you *make* me leave," I said.

Her eyes flashed a bright blue showing her wolf to me. Her scent strengthened and whirled around me. I'd turned the shewolf's hormones upside down. She didn't know what to do with herself. "I could," she said, pushing on my chest.

I took her hand which strained against mine, but I didn't let go. I lifted it to my lips and kissed her fingertips. "No, you couldn't," I said.

"Let me go," she hissed. I obliged her, then enjoyed the view of her ass as she hurried inside to get away from the only man that had turned her on tonight. The door slammed on the house, and it shook with the vibration.

"Well, that was kinda hot," Sully said

"You are gay. She didn't do anything for you," I said with a grin.

"No, but her scent is strong. Right, Mal?"

"It is very strong," Malphas said.

"I do that to her. No one else," I said.

"Well, don't you have it all figured out?" Sully teased.

"Shut-up and get in the vehicle," I snapped. He wasn't going to dim my mood now. Lyra still wanted me, and she knew I wasn't leaving. I did wonder what she and James were up to, but I wanted to check out Orange Grove before I let her in on our information.

TWELVE

THE DRIVE between Dog River and Orange Grove was boring. Night had consumed us, and we drove in the darkness to a town I'd never heard of before now. Malphas rode with us instead of flying. Sully slept in the seat behind mine while Mal's dark eyes watched the road for deer and other animals. It was cool outside, and they would be moving. We rode in silence as I covered what we knew in my head.

My mother, Araxia, owned many casinos across the country. She had been the contact person to the packs while I still lived in Louisiana. The traffickers used the port in Steelshore to funnel fairies from one place through a pipeline built with the packs of the southern United States. Somehow there were three red cloaked witches involved. I believed that Henri had seen them. Lyra's pack had been targeted, but I didn't understand why. Araxia went after male Alphas, but with the news of an Alpha coming to takeover another pack, I wondered what other powers were involved.

There were reasons why Faeborn wolves had bad reputations. They represented when the race of fairies meddled in wolf business. We were a strong and powerful race. Mixing their blood with ours gave an already ferocious entity a stronger force. With their meddling, I wonder how many purebred wolves were left in the southern packs. I hadn't sensed a single Faeborn wolf in Dog River.

"No Faeborn!" I said.

"What?" Sully said, waking up with my sudden exclamation.

"There are no Faeborn wolves in Dog River. Did you sense any?" I asked.

"No. They are a pure pack," he said.

"Are they the last pure pack?" I asked.

"Probably one of the last," he said. "What difference does that make?"

"If the fairies are trying to destroy the purity of the race, there has to be a reason. An advantage to them somehow. What would it be?" I asked.

"A wolf can go head to head with a fairy, but a Faeborn wolf is stronger," he said.

"Can they control us? Can our mother control us because we have her blood in us? Like Grace controls the fairies?" I asked.

"I don't know, but Grace's power is found in the willingness of her people to follow her. It's not because she takes it by force. These packs are being forced into fairy rule. Our packs were tricked into it. They must have realized what she was doing after my father's death. The wolves are resisting her. If she wanted to control us, she could have kept us in Houma," he said.

"Long game," I muttered.

"Fairies always play the long game," Malphas said.

"Turn on the left ahead. We have about two hours before sunrise. There is an abandoned house where Echo is waiting for us up on the right."

I followed his directions to a house that had seen better days. Parking in front with the F.B.I. logo emblazoned on the side of the vehicle, I knew no one would question it. We found Echo inside. He began to sign frantically. Malphas calmed him down. I'd never seen him so upset.

"What's wrong?" I asked, missing most of the signs.

"He says that he thinks they know we are here. He's worried about Dog River," Malphas said.

"Then we go back," I replied.

"We need to know what is going on," Sully countered.

"Then you stay!" I snapped at him. His brow furrowed. "I'm sorry. It's just that they are back there without us."

"Do you believe that Lyra is capable of leading her pack or not?" Sully asked.

"You are digging that hole deeper," I replied.

"So, the answer is yes, but you still want to be the hero," Sully replied.

"I want to be what she needs!" I shouted back. The rafters of the old house rattled.

"She needs you to be here," Malphas said quietly. I looked up to Echo who signed that it would be okay. "We will take to the air in an hour to see if we can catch them coming up from Biloxi. You and Sully should glamour yourselves."

"They aren't expecting any Faeborn. That is, if my theory about the pure packs is true," I said.

"Then, it better be a damn good glamour," Malphas replied. He had a little fire in his voice. Whatever was bothering Echo, now bothered him. "We need to be able to communicate."

"How do we do that?" I asked.

Sully had found a spot against a mostly solid wall and sat down on the dusty wooden floor.

"I will need you to bond with me," Malphas said.

"Blood bond?" I asked. He nodded, then sliced his hand open with a knife that looked like a black feather. He handed it to me, and I did the same. Before I let him clasp my hand, I asked. "Am I going to regret this?"

"Probably," he said with a devilish grin. He slapped his hand in mine and tilted his head back which shifted partially to a raven. Feathers formed on his cheeks and across his brow. He opened his mouth, releasing a loud caw that rattled in my head. He jerked his hand away from me and stared.

"Is that it?" I asked.

He backed away from me and pushed Echo back, too. Sully perked up and stood.

"What's happening?" he asked.

"They are talking to each other," I replied, watching Malphas' eyes twitch wildly in his head like he was in a deep sleep, dreaming, but with his eyes wide open.

Echo's telepathic voice broke the silence. I grabbed my ears as it hissed in my head. *"You are the moon dog who will snatch the orb from the sky and consume it. You will devour the bodies of the dead. Your mother, the giantess, will laugh and call us all fools."*

Malphas collapsed to the ground, and Echo knelt next to him. I fell to my knees and grabbed his shoulder.

"What the fuck was that?" I asked.

"He saw you. He saw her," he signed slow enough for me to read.

"What does that mean?" I begged. "Is he alright?"

"He will be fine. As to what it means, I do not know. I saw what he saw. You were no longer yourself or your wolf. You were a warg," he said.

"What is a warg?" I asked.

"Those big wolf things on Lord of the Rings that the orcs were riding," Sully said. Echo shook his head in disgust.

"No. Not fiction," he signed, as he held Malphas' head in his lap.

"Oh, so he's a warg that can look through the eyes of other animals," Sully said.

"I thought I said not fiction," I translated for Echo who was becoming agitated again. "It's okay, Echo. You don't have to explain," I told him.

"Give me a moment. His head is still full of visions," he replied.

"No, it can't be," Sully muttered.

"Can't be what?" I asked, keeping my eyes on Malphas.

"It's just a legend," he said.

"Sully, I swear," I snapped at him again.

"Rougarou," Sully said.

"That's a legend," I replied.

The Rougarou was a bi-pedal werewolf that haunted the swamps of Louisiana. Even the common wolves like my father would tell us to avoid the curse howl of the beast. I'd never heard it myself.

"We have a festival every year in Houma for the Rougarou legends. It has always been said that it was a Faeborn wolf that lost its mind," Sully said.

"You believe this nonsense?" I asked.

"Honestly, Brother, I have always believed that there were those of us who couldn't handle the class of the dual blood that flows in our veins. When I first saw you and heard about your wandering, I considered that you might have been one. Maybe you are," Sully said.

"Bullshit," I responded. "Is a Rougarou a warg?"

Echo lifted his eyes to meet mine. "Yes."

"And he thinks I'm that?" I asked, standing up away from them.

"He is still showing me his vision. I do not know if it was you, but your blood triggered it. The wargs of our people were the sons of gods which were nothing other than fairies. Wargs could shift and be bi-pedal. They also have a thirst for blood. Fenrir is a warg," Echo signed.

"The hellhound?"

"Not necessarily, but he can bring about the end of the world," Echo signed back to me.

"I shift into a wolf." I shifted quickly. My clothes shredded with the shift, and I hit the floor on all fours. Sully reached over and patted me on the head. I snarled at him, then shifted back, glamouring clothes to wear. "Don't fucking pet me."

"You looked like you needed some brotherly encouragement," Sully said. "Plus, you are such a good boy."

I growled at him, and he laughed at me. "I'm not some evil, world ending, man wolf."

Malphas stirred, and Echo helped him to sit up. "You can shift like that," Malphas said with clarity. "And if you let it happen when you don't have control. You will kill us all. I have seen it."

"Since when did you do oracly things?" Sully asked.

"I can see thought," he responded.

"Those were not my thoughts," I protested.

"No, but it is your subconscious. That is inside of you whether it can take physical form or not. I do not know," Malphas said as Echo helped him stand. "We've wasted time. We must fly. I will speak to you now."

"Speak to me?" I asked.

I'd forgotten about the bond when his voice rattled my brain. *"You can hear me now."*

"Yes."

"Respond in your head. Otherwise you will look like a madman." His voice had a hint of amusement in it.

"*Yes. I hear you. When this is done, you will tell me everything that you saw,*" I demanded.

"*Nick, what I saw does not change who you are.*"

"*You will tell me,*" I reinforced. He nodded in response, then exited the dilapidated house with Echo. They burst into a cloud of feathers and flew away.

"What did he say?" Sully asked.

"He told me what he saw doesn't change who I am," I said.

"That sucks. I was hoping you'd turn into something cool for once." I punched him in the shoulder. "See, so violent. What's lurking under your skin?" he teased.

"You got a good glamour for this?" I asked.

"Of course, I do. I'm fabulous. Besides, I've travelled the south from town to town. I change my look with each new place," he said. Then his visage warbled, and my dirty blond-haired brother morphed into a man with dark brown hair and a beard with an extra bit of weight around the middle. I pulled out my phone and took a quick picture. "What are you doing?"

"Saving it for Callum," I said.

"You mother fucker!"

"Blackmail, baby!" I said, as I morphed into a plain fellow with black hair and dark eyes.

"You are boring. At least I have flair."

"Flair and a couple of extra doughnuts." I stuck my finger in his belly. He giggled like a dough boy. "Malphas in my head is weird."

"Is he talking now?"

"Yes, he said that we need to get moving. The caravan is already on the outskirts of town."

We walked into the center of the small city. A group of people had gathered around a man who was speaking to the townsfolk.

"Don't worry. Perhaps this will be a good thing. We haven't had an Alpha since Joseph died last year," the man said.

"No outsiders!" someone shouted.

"Tell them to go away!" another added.

We remained along the edges of the crowd. If anyone looked too long at us, we moved away. More people showed up as the sun rose, and within thirty minutes, the caravan arrived. Malphas and Echo sat in a nearby tree.

There were three black cars with deeply tinted windows. Using my sight, I could see the fairy power filling each vehicle. Two men stepped out of the front vehicle and walked to the second car. A man who reminded me of Tennyson Schuyler stepped out of the vehicle. He wore a tailored suit, but tattoos crawled up his neck and down over his hands. His dark blue eyes scanned the crowd. He took a pair of aviator sunglasses and put them on despite the cloudy day.

Several other men exited the vehicle, and the group walked to the man who had been speaking. They shook hands. I was shocked that I didn't recognize this man. Looking through my sight, I wanted to see if it was a glamour. I could only see the bright blue hue making him a Winter fairy.

"*Do you know him?*" I asked Malphas.

"*I've never seen him,*" he responded.

"Who is this guy? He makes Tennyson look a pussy," Sully muttered.

"Don't draw attention," I warned.

The hulking man looked over the crowd as if he already owned them. Instinctively, the crowd parted for him, lowering their heads in reverence. He shook hands with the man who had been speaking to the crowd.

"I am Sirius Nashoba, your new Alpha," he said. One by one the men and women of Orange Grove knelt before this man. Even those who had voiced their concerns hit their knees without protest. We followed suit and bowed before the man. "I am the spirit of all wolves. I am the beginning of the wolf and if you test me, I will be your end. The Orange Grove pack is under my protection. I designate Ishmael Barnabe to be my Beta for this area. As he speaks, so I speak." He laid his hand on the shoulder of the man who had announced the Alpha's arrival. We continued to kneel waiting for him to give us the order to stand. However, he did not. He walked through the kneeling crowd, stopping before the women in the group.

"To cement his commitment to the pack, Alpha Nashoba will choose a female from the pack and provide us with our own future heir," Barnabe said.

"You!" Nashoba pointed down at a young woman who couldn't be much older than twenty. She shook as he pointed at her. "Stand up." The woman rose keeping her face to the ground. I'd heard of packs that had overbearing Alphas, but I thought such overt reverence had faded away. This pack seemed to be trained for it. "Do you accept the offer to bear the heir for your pack?"

"Yes, my Alpha," she replied.

"No!" a voice growled near us.

The Alpha's eyes snapped toward the area where we knelt. He stomped through the crowd to a young man who kept his head down. He jerked the man from his position by his collar.

"No?" he asked. His eyes began to glow a bright blue.

The young man shook, but he explained himself. "She is my betrothed."

"Good. You shall raise my child after I have blessed this pack with it," he said, slamming the man back down to the ground. Something snapped loudly, and the man grabbed his leg. I'd had my fair share of broken bones, so I knew the noise. "Thank me."

"Thank you, Alpha," the man said while grinding his teeth in pain.

"Come with me," he said, curling his finger to the woman. She followed him willingly. Sully flinched next to me, and I grabbed his arm.

"No," I muttered.

"You are going to let her go with that brute."

"She consented. Had she told him no, I would have intervened," I said.

"That is not consent. She had no choice. You know that," Sully scolded.

"If we do this now, we will lose Dog River. He will take a woman from there. Could you imagine if he chose Tinley? She's nearly the same age as that woman," I said. "Please, Brother."

"It's wrong," Sully said.

"I know it is," I replied. "I know. Well, fuck." I'd have Malphas and Echo follow them. I feared that if we intervened it would doom any chance that we have at stopping them with Dog River. *"Follow them. We will be close behind. Perhaps we can get the girl back."*

"I would advise against it," Malphas reasoned.

"I would, too."

THIRTEEN

SULLY FOLLOWED the caravan but left at least a mile between us. Malphas and Echo flew above the vehicle. I watched as Malphas dipped low, coasting over the middle vehicle.

"*It's more than consent,*" he said in my head.

"*What do you mean?*"

"*They have already been together. She didn't tell her betrothed. They are already swapping gravy in the car,*" Malphas said.

I couldn't help myself. I began to laugh despite the seriousness of the situation. Malphas' raven voice in my head using Levi's term for having sex struck me as odd and hilarious.

"What's so funny?" Sully grumped.

"We can slow down. He's already been with her before today. Malphas said they are doing it in the back of the car," I said.

"Why is that funny?"

"Because he said they were swapping gravy," I said.

Sully pulled the SUV over to the side of the road. "What?"

"It means having sex."

"I get that."

"Levi started it."

"It's ridiculous," he said. "So, we aren't saving the girl."

"It seems we aren't, but it doesn't stop me from worrying about Tinley."

"Why wouldn't you worry about Lyra?"

"Really? That man couldn't handle her."

"You can't either," Sully pointed out.

"True. Let's go back to Dog River. She needs to know what happened here. I'll get Levi on finding out what he can about Sirius Nashoba."

Sully turned the vehicle around, and we headed east toward Alabama. When he did, we almost ran over Malphas and Echo who stood in the middle of the road in human form. They climbed into the back of the vehicle.

"We are tired," Malphas said.

"Okay," I responded as I fished out my phone to call Levi. Of course, the voice that answered wasn't Levi.

"Well, hello, you rogue bastard," Grace said.

"My Queen," I flattered her.

"You know I am going to jerk a knot in your tail for calling me that," she smirked.

"As much as I'd love to talk to you and that smart mouth, I called to talk to Levi," I said.

"Oh, so you'd rather talk to his smart mouth," she said.

"I always knew he was a smart man. I don't need to know what he does with it. I just need to talk to him," I responded.

"Aren't you precious? I suppose I can allow you to speak to the king. How's the woman?" she asked.

"Don't want to talk about that," I said.

"Need help? I can give you pointers," she said.

"Grace, I'm pretty sure that nothing you could say would help the situation."

"Don't underestimate my powers, Dominick Meyer," she said. "How's Sully?"

"Grace! Can I talk to Levi?"

"I'm fine," Sully said. His wolf hearing was good enough to hear her even though she wasn't on speaker phone.

"See! Was that so hard?"

"I swear to the Tree there are too many difficult women in my life," I said.

"Perhaps that is your problem, Nick. Some women enjoy the undivided attention of one man. Here's Levi," she said.

"And that's your Grace wisdom of the day. Hey, what's up?" Levi asked. I paused, allowing Grace's words to sink in. Lyra probably thought I was going back to Steelshore. I'd even said I was, once we solved their problem. She wouldn't invest any emotions into us, because I'd straight up told her that I wasn't staying. I'd have to give up moving to Birmingham to head up the central operations of the Fairy Bureau of Immigration. "Nick?"

"Sorry."

Levi chuckled. "She got to you."

"No comment. Look, we just came across a guy down here named Sirius Nashoba. He's definitely Winter by his aura. I need to know if you have anything on him. He called himself the Spirit of the Wolf. He's the Alpha that the fairies are placing in the small packs here. Dog River is next," I said.

"I'll look it up. Anything else?"

"Do you know anything about a Rougarou?" I asked.

"Unfortunately," he said.

"Really?"

"Yeah, when I was with she who will not be named, they used my power to summon the demon. There was a strong coven of creole witches there. One of them was a man that was a Rougarou. It's like a witchy warlocky wolf man," he explained. "Have you met one?"

"Malphas had a vision of one," I said, leaving it at that.

"Well, you probably want to steer clear of it. Outside of Lisette, he was probably the most powerful thing there. We are still working on the red cloak thing. I don't have much to report," he said.

"Thanks for everything, Levi," I said. "Tell Grace thanks, too."

"I'd rather not," he replied with a laugh and hung up the phone.

"Well, he pretty much cut me off," I said.

"We need powerful," Sully said.

"I'm not a Rougarou. Besides wouldn't that make you one, too? Perhaps the Rougarou is nothing more than a Faeborn fairy," I said.

"Well, when either one of us walks bipedal in wolf form, then I'll subscribe to it," he said. "But you should probably teach me some of that fairy shit before we face Sirius."

"I can do that."

We rode in silence from that point back to the small hotel in Dog River. Maybe I wasn't ready to give up my plans. There wasn't anything wrong with that. But I couldn't have my cake and eat it, too. I had to decide and stop expecting her to act on the feelings that I knew she had.

Malphas and Echo returned to their room next to ours,

and I sat on the end of the bed deep in thought when there was a knock on the door.

Sully opened it to find James standing there.

"I need your help," he said, looking at me.

"With what?" I asked.

"She's down at the bar, and she won't listen to me," he said.

"Drunk?" I asked.

He sighed. "You can't think that she does this often. She doesn't. She's just lost right now. I think you can get to her. At the very least, order her to go home."

"I can't order her to do anything. I wouldn't do it anyway. But let me grab my helmet." It sat on a stool next to the bathroom. I looked at myself in the mirror. I looked tired, but if she needed me, I would be there.

I followed James' truck to the bar on my motorcycle. When I walked inside with him, I saw her immediately. She sat on the bar, swinging her legs like a kid.

"Why don't you get down from there, Lyra," Hector said.

She giggled at him, then her face fell when she saw me. "Well, looky here, our savior has returned!"

From the patrons inside the bar, I got the impression that they were tired of her antics. James stood beside me, and she showed her fangs at him.

"You are in the dog house," I said.

"It's the price of having a best friend like Lyra," he replied.

"Best friend," I said.

"Well, she has Aspen, too, but we figured our relationship was good on the friend part. We never could get the love part right," he admitted.

"I suppose I don't have to kill you now," I said.

"Nope. She's all yours," he said. He meant it literally

because he turned and left me standing alone in the bar face to face with a drunk Alpha female. I had two options. I could placate her and try to sweet talk her which wouldn't work. Or I could be the bad guy and out Alpha her Alpha. Neither choice would get me anywhere with her. The stress had worn on her long enough that she'd given into using alcohol to ease her nerves. If I had to guess, she probably wasn't that drunk. Every Alpha I'd ever known knew how to drink anyone under a table, but I suppose she could have been three sheets to the wind.

"I'm going to regret this," I muttered as I marched toward her.

"Big bad Alpha. Look at him," she tilted her head back and laughed. I knew then that she wasn't as drunk as she was pretending to be. I didn't slow down until I'd spread her knees and placed my body between her legs.

"I know you aren't as drunk as you are pretending to be, so why don't you get down from there. We can go talk about it," I said.

"Passive aggressive has never been a turn-on for me," she replied. The others in the room watched from their places, but not directly.

"I know what turns you on, and I'm not offering it," I said. "Get down and let's go home."

She pressed her finger into my chest. "You don't get to tell me what to do. You can join James on my shit list."

"I want to be at the top of it," I replied.

"Then you'd have to drag me out of this bar by force."

"You asked for it," I said. Pulling on the force of Winter like Levi had taught me, I wrapped my arms around her waist, hauled her off the bar, and tossed her over my shoulder. She began to kick and scream.

"Put me down, you moron!" She pounded her fists into

my back, but the power that I'd drawn in protected me from pain. The people in the bar laughed.

"I won't hurt her. If anyone doubts that, you're welcome to follow us as I take her home," I said.

Lyra continued to kick and scream as we walked into the parking lot. I sat her down next to my motorcycle. She tried to bolt, but I hauled her back to me.

"Stop! I need to run!"

"Then, I'll run with you," I said.

"No. Let me go!" she said, beating on my chest.

"You don't have time to do this after what I saw today. Your pack is about to be lost to the fairies. Do you want that?" I asked.

"We can't stop it!" she yelled at me.

"We will fight it," I said.

"You have a death wish. Now let me go, Nick! Are you getting some kind of pervy thrill out of this! I know you are!"

With that, I let her go and stepped away from her. "No, I'm not. I do not want to see you destroy yourself. I do not want anything to happen to Tinley. You have to be strong for her and your pack."

"Don't lecture me. You abandoned your pack! You will abandon us, too," she shouted.

Mustering what magic I could, I placed it behind my oath. "I swear to you, Lyra Rochon, that I will never abandon Dog River or you." The trees shook, and the ground beneath our feet rumbled.

She turned on her heel and darted into the woods. She shifted just before she hit the tree line and like a fool. I followed her.

Lyra and I had run once before as wolves, but I didn't remember her being this fast. She dashed between trees and through thickets of bushes faster than I could keep up.

Eventually, I lost her. She might know the terrain better than me, but I knew her scent. It surrounded me as I ran. Using it as my compass, I ran into a large clearing filled with tall grass. She stood in the center of it, looking up at the stars.

Naked and stunning. Her hair flowed in the wind as the moon rose above us, almost full.

"You are too slow, Alpha," she said.

I shifted and glamoured a set of clothes. No need to assume I was getting a piece of her fine, naked ass.

"You are impressive, Alpha," I said, returning the moniker.

"My problem is I can't create clothes out of nothing," she said, turning to me.

As a wolf, nakedness wasn't unusual to me, but Lyra's nakedness was something I'd never get used to. I kept my distance, but she walked closer to me.

"I can do it for you, but I really don't want to," I replied, testing the waters.

"You created your own. I assumed you weren't interested in being naked with me."

"I don't assume anything with you," I replied.

"Good for you." She walked up to me. I may not have twitched outwardly, but everything inside of me sat on the edge of a cliff waiting to jump. Willing to plunge to that death. She laid her hand on my chest. I released the magic creating my shirt. Her warm palm laid on my bare skin. "So, if I touch it, it disappears?"

"Only if you want," I replied.

"What do you want?" she asked.

"I gave you my oath."

"Your oath didn't tell me what you wanted."

"What I want doesn't matter. It never has."

"You have never done anything for selfish reasons?"

she asked, allowing her hand to drop down to my side just above the line of my jeans. The internal twitching ramped up to a vibrating hum.

"I have. Nothing I'm proud of."

"When you first met me, was that for selfish reasons?"

Her question puzzled me. "Do you want it to be? I'm getting mixed signals, and I'll be honest, I'm not good with that shit."

She slid her hand down over the top of my jeans, hooking her fingers in the belt loops. I did not release the magic. Something inside said I was being set up. Something was wrong.

"Your instincts are better than I thought they would be," she said.

I stepped away from her. I reached out with my senses and looked around us in the darkness with my sight. Several figures moved in the darkness.

"What did you do?" I asked.

"I made a deal. Tinley, my aunts, and the packs will be safe," she said.

"For me?"

"He asked for you," she said. "I'm sorry, Nick. But I'd do anything to keep my family safe. It doesn't matter how I feel if you are the thing standing between us and autonomy."

I stepped back to her and pulled her closer to me. "This is a mistake. You know that, right? They will never let you keep the pack. They are just getting me out of the way."

"Creed gave his word. They knew you were in Orange Grove and approached me while you were gone. It seems he has an old vendetta that he's wanting to settle. In exchange for you, I get to keep my pack. You gave your oath back there. Dog River needs you to go with them. It's the price for our freedom. I know you have family. I know the Queen is your benefactor. I'll pay whatever price she demands, even if it is my life. I'll do *anything* to keep Tinley safe."

"That's enough explanation. You had your time, She Wolf," Creed said behind me. I'd heard him move up closer to me. "Long time, no see, Dominick Meyer."

"Fuck off, Creed."

"It's funny, because like a moron you gave her your oath, so you have to come with us willingly."

I didn't turn to look at him. I kept my eyes fixed on Lyra. She'd betrayed me, but I didn't feel betrayed. I felt sorry that she felt like she had to make this decision to save her pack. It broke my heart that it was a ruse, and they would take it easily from her without us here to help her.

"*Malphas!*"

"*What the fuck? I should have cut you off! Can't I sleep?*"

"*Whine more, Birdbrain. Lyra sold me out to Creed Davis with promises to leave the pack alone. I'm going with them because I gave my word to her. My oath.*"

"*You are an idiot.*"

"*Thanks. Make sure that Sully doesn't come after me. He needs to stay here and keep Tinley safe. Call in reinforcements. She can get pissed if she wants to now. I don't give a fuck. We are not letting this pack fall to Araxia.*"

"*You know I can't keep him from coming after you.*"

"*Tell him that if anything happens to Tinley, I am holding him personally responsible.*"

"*Alright. We are in the air. Unfortunately, I can feel where you are.*"

"What's he doing?" Creed asked.

Lyra tilted her head, and I winked at her. "I'm sorry," she muttered.

"Ain't no thing," I said, backing away from her to where I knew Creed waited to restrain me. I would go willingly. She needed to learn who to trust. Creed and his ilk couldn't hurt me. Not anymore. I wasn't the weak child he'd picked on back in Whiskey Chito, my old pack.

I watched a tear roll down her cheek, and as it dripped from her chin to her bare skin. My feelings for Lyra Rochon evaporated. My wolf protested inside of me. It wanted to run. It sensed the danger, but I controlled the wolf. Not the other way around.

"Your mother will be so happy to see you," Creed said as he snapped a pair of handcuffs on my wrists. I felt the fairy power in them to restrain me. Unfortunately for him, when it was time, I'd take off my cuff and tear him to shreds.

Before I took my eyes off Lyra, I warned her. "You listen to me. This will not save your pack. Do whatever you have to do to keep Tinley safe."

James walked out of the forest with a set of clothes for Lyra. He'd been in on it. Best friends forever. They could both fuck off, but I'd included Dog River in my oath. This wasn't over by any stretch of the imagination.

FOURTEEN

JUST BEFORE CREED put me in a car, I saw Malphas land in a tree across the road from us. I didn't want to zone out and talk to him. I was dealing with Creed who I knew now to be as much a Faeborn wolf as I was.

"You know, you've been trouble since you were born," he said.

"I'm not done yet," I replied.

"Now, now. I can't have you running back to help Miss Rochon and her pack. Too bad she fell for our proposal. You are right. We will be back with in 48 hours, and the last pure pack of wolves in the South will be ours."

"Why does it matter?" I asked. He was talking. I might as well get as much information as possible.

"I'm not telling you, and I can't have you contacting your fairy friends in Shady Grove," he said.

Levi. I could talk to Levi. I'd sworn myself to him. I drew power as quickly as I could. I felt Creed moving behind me. My mind connected to Levi. Thankfully, he was in Shady Grove and not Winter. I wouldn't have been able to reach him there. It was almost as though I felt him cock his head as I reached out to him through my blood oath to him and Grace.

"Levi. Call Sully. Trouble..."

Unfortunately, that was all I got before Creed knocked me out.

~

When I woke up, the sun blasted my face. I jerked but didn't move far. I'd been restrained while sitting up in an office chair. I felt the choking control of a magical collar around my neck.

"Fuck," I muttered.

"Watch your language, Son."

My eyes focused on the dark-haired, gorgeous woman sitting across from me. Memories flooded my mind of being a scared child whose father tried to pawn him off to a mother he'd never met. I remembered standing in the forest that day and hating both of them. I no longer hated my father. It was hard to hate the dead. But this woman. This fairy. I could hate her. Hate seethed out of my pores for her.

"I'm surprised that I'm alive," I said.

"Why?" she asked. It didn't matter how beautiful she was. She would always be uglier than a monkey's armpit to me.

"Seems you like to kill men," I replied.

She leaned back in the chair on the other side of an ornate desk. Outside the window I could see the Gulf of Mexico. They'd taken me to the casino in Biloxi. I felt the wards in the room. I also felt every single Faeborn wolf in the room. I wondered if they were all her offspring. Her make-shift family. I claimed none of them.

"Dearest Dominick, you are more like me than you know. I have special plans for you, and that collar will make sure that you do them. You see, when we go back to Dog River to present them with their new Alpha, it's going to be you. You will go in there and defile the last pure pack in the Southern United States, because I'll order you to take Lyra Rochon as your mate. You've already established the connection. She didn't need much encouragement the night I pointed you out to her at the bar. Of course, she didn't know you were my son, nor did she realize that you were a wolf. A little persuasion goes a long way."

"I won't do it."

"That collar says you will."

"If you think this collar can hold me, then you will be surprised," I said.

"It was made specifically for you. It contains your blood. You gave it willingly when you attacked Rocco. He came back to us with everything I needed. Hair. Blood. A wicked little spell. And now you will do my bidding," she replied.

"Is Rocco another one of your offspring?" I asked.

"No, he is not. He is a Faeborn wolf as is his father, but he is not mine. In fact, it might surprise you that I only have two sets of children. Two sets of triplets," she replied. "I knew from the moment that you, your brother, and your sister were born, that you would be the strongest of the three. That is why I placed you with a dying pack and a dying Alpha. I kept Sullivan and Suzanna with me to keep an eye on them. They were fine until they met you."

I tried to piece together what she was saying. "They are my half-siblings."

"No."

"No?"

"You and they are the product of my blood and the

blood of the former Houma Alpha, Hiram Talbot. Such a shame about Hiram. I really did like him."

"And Frank Meyer?" I asked.

"Poor Francisco. He was shooting blanks. Like I said, it was a dying pack and a dying Alpha. He couldn't have children if he tried," she said.

"They were pregnant before me, and the child died," I said.

"Yes, well, Regina Meyer's first love was none other than Creed Martin. She lost his child," Araxia said. Creed walked from behind me to her side. "And he has been my faithful servant ever since. I promised him retribution for being cut off from his child. He also made sure that you were toughened up while living in Whiskey Chito. Your travels did the rest. Now, I have a street hardy, Alpha male to place in power. It's a shame about your hand though."

I suddenly realized my cuff was gone. My hand and stub were tied to the chair behind me. I was so caught up in her revelations that I didn't realize it was gone. She picked it up from the desk and hummed.

"I would like to have that back," I said.

"You don't need it. The collar will provide you with my magic to conjure your glamoured hand. I've been told you lost it saving the life of the new Winter Queen. Is that true?" she asked.

"What does it matter? It's gone," I said.

"I'd like to meet her one day. She and I have many things to discuss. I'm sure you have questions, Dominick. You may ask them. This will be your only chance to get the answers you want," she said.

I hated her for offering. I had questions. Hundreds of them, but I didn't want to give her the satisfaction of knowing that. I did have one that I felt was important, not just to me.

"Why the trafficking?" I asked.

"Oh, that's just a side business. Everything I do is about power. There is gold involved, but with every fairy that I sell, that customer becomes beholden to me. They offer me reverence for my product. They make me that much stronger until the day I can take back what is rightfully mine."

"And what is that?"

"Everything," she replied. "Take him down to the holding cells and feed him. He looks too skinny to me."

"I'll be happy to, my Lady," Creed responded.

"Not you. You and your son are to stay away from him. He's no longer your enemy. He's my son and will be our greatest asset when he realizes his potential. Mr. Handley, would you please take my son to the cells."

I turned as far as I could in my seat. I expected to see Sly Handley, Michael's father. We hadn't seen much of him since the end of the war. Instead, there sat Callum's boyfriend, Michael.

"You fucking traitor," I snarled at him.

"It's not like that, Nick," he said.

"What is it like? You bastard. You wait until I tell him what a rat you are!" I yelled.

"Son, calm down," Araxia said.

Michael moved to roll the chair I was sitting in, but I managed to get my stub loose, thus loosening the ropes enough to get my other arm free. I spun in the chair, knocking Michael to the ground. With a quick claw to the rope on my feet, I was on him in an instant. My hands worked faster than my mind pummeling him.

"You are a traitor!" I screamed.

"Down!" Araxia screamed. A stream of lightning shocked my body, and I fell to the side, twitching in pain. "You made me do that!"

I couldn't answer her, but I saw the horror in Michael's eyes. He knew the moment I was loose that he was a dead man. I didn't care if he was Callum's boyfriend or not. I was going to rip his head off. "I'm going to kill you."

"Such violence. Anger. Hatred. Yes, I love my children, but you, dear Dominick, are my pride and joy," Araxia said, standing over me. "Stand!" My legs and feet despite the painful shocks forced me to stand. "I might as well do it myself. Follow."

Step by step, I followed behind my mother. She'd pointed Michael out on purpose. She knew I would react. I wasn't the kind soul like Sully. Nor the harsh, but loveable smart-mouthed Suzi. I'd suppressed my anger. I'd held back my fears and doubts. She'd reminded me of all of them, and I'd lost my head, going after him. Maybe she was right. Maybe I was just her son.

~

They fed me like a king. Steak, potatoes, salad. All of which I had to eat with my hands. I supposed I was more barbarian than king. I tried connecting to Malphas and Levi, but whatever ward Araxia had around the place kept magic from getting out or in. There were no windows in my cell. I wondered why a casino would have concrete cells with pressurized doors, but I supposed they were good for keeping werewolves and whatever else she kept down here.

Her explanation about the trafficking didn't make sense. I understood the concept of vowed or oathed authority. If I'd made an oath to Grace and Levi, that oath made them more powerful because my will would coincide with theirs. But a simple transaction or an exchange of goods didn't seem like it would derive enough power to amount to anything.

She didn't even feel like my mother. Not that I knew what that felt like anyway. I was a means to an end for her. I didn't expect to be loved or coddled. I don't know what I expected. Sitting down on the cot they'd provided. I looked up to the ceiling and closed my eyes. My ears popped as someone opened the door.

Michael stepped through the opening, and the door shut behind him. His face looked like a plum. Apparently, I didn't hit him hard enough since he was still walking around. I'd went head to head with fairies before.

"Back for more?" I asked.

"She's saving the packs," he said.

"Take your brainwashed bullshit and get the fuck out."

"I know he won't understand, but I've been protecting him."

"Are you still talking?" I finally stood up to face him. "Get out. If I'm going to be a prisoner, I'm going to push for solitary. If you open your mouth again, I'm going to take your teeth out with my fist."

He pressed his lips together and winced. He wanted to say more, but he also knew I didn't intend on listening to his crap. He made the smart move and walked out of the room. I sat back down on the bed as the door shut.

"You look like shit," a truly glorious voice echoed around me.

"Why thank you, my Queen." I looked around the room, and Grace giggled. Only she would giggle when I was stuck in a prison and collar. She shimmered into view near the door.

"How the hell did you get in here? And you shouldn't be here," I said.

"Well, Michael's activities haven't gone unnoticed, and

when Callum said he didn't come home last night, I knew something was up. And when two of my servants get into it, I know," she said, walking over to me. Her turquoise eyes glittered with Winter power. She practically vibrated with it. How she was doing it within the wards, I had no idea. But I was damn glad to see her. "I kinda like the collar. Rufus is so bad sometimes; I think I need a new dog."

"Woof," I said. Her sass was infectious. It made me realize how much I missed Shady Grove and my pack and family there.

"May I?" she asked, reaching for the collar.

"Please take it off. I need to get back to Dog River," I said. The cool touches of her fingertips brushed over my skin, making me shiver. Her brow furrowed. "What is it?"

"I can't take it off. Not here. I can in Winter, but it's strong. Is this your mother?" she asked.

"Yes," I replied. "What do we do?"

"I can change the power behind it. She wouldn't be able to control you, but as long as you play along, she won't notice," she said.

"Who will control me?"

"I think you know the answer to that."

"You are shitting me. You are just joking, right? Grace, you already have my blood oath. Why are you toying with me?"

Her eyes darkened. "Nick, I swear on my crown. I can't take it off which is very concerning. You either deal with me as your master or her."

She was serious. She couldn't take it off, and I saw the look in her eyes. That was bad. It meant that in this place, my mother was stronger than she. Now, Grace had a ton of power behind her, and by the Tree, they would tear this place to shreds if my mother made a move.

"She said you had things to discuss," I said.

"I'm sure we do, but not today. I leave the collar. Change the power. You go with her back to Dog River and save that pack. I'll send reinforcements. You are going to need it."

"No, Lyra doesn't want that."

"I should slap you."

"What?!"

"She betrayed you. Quit using your dick to make your decisions," she scolded.

"It's not my dick," I said.

She shook her head. "Fucking hearts."

"Tell me about it. I don't trust her. I can't. Probably not ever again, but I made an oath not to turn my back on that pack. I won't do it. Even if that means breaking my oath to you," I said, waiting for her rebuke.

Instead, she kissed my cheek. "For a broken man, you've got one hell of a heart, Dominick Meyer."

"I take after my Queen," I said. She laid her hands on the collar. Power swirled around us in a cold blizzard wind. Her platinum locks floated outward from her head and her eyes glowed a brilliant blue.

With one word that power rushed to the collar. "Mine."

She pulled away, but I grabbed her hand. "Don't let Callum stay with him."

"Callum knows. He chose to keep tabs on Michael. Thank you for your concern for my son. Or is it concern for your brother?" she asked. Damn. Grace always knew everything. A smile spread across her face. "I know you can do this, but we are here. You make the call and we will come. I'll bring all of Winter with me if I have to. You are *my* knight, and I don't take that lightly."

"Thank you."

She smiled, then faded away. I didn't think I'd ever

understand Grace, and I probably didn't want to. I sat down on the cot again, feeling the freedom of her control swirling around my neck. I could breathe again.

Two men I didn't know ran into the room. "Where is she?"

"Who?" I asked. My mother's alarms had picked up Grace.

"The Winter Queen!"

"Let me tell you something, if she was here, it would take more than you two punks to take her out. You better be glad she isn't here," I said.

The one on the right hit his radio. "Nothing here, Boss."

"Sight?" the radio voice squawked back.

"Nothing magical here except his collar," he answered.

"Alright. Get out of there before the wolf takes off your head," the radio man said.

"You heard him," I said. I didn't dare conjure my claws or any other abilities.

I settled back and focused on Malphas' vision. It certainly seemed like the tales of the Rougarou from my childhood. The monstrous wolf walked upright and ate people. I might have had the taste for blood occasionally, but never to eat. A woman in my old pack told me she'd seen the Rougarou once. She said he had red glowing eyes and 2-foot claws that tore through flesh like a hot knife through butter. Even Sully had seemed adamant that the Rougarou was a real thing.

Of course, I lived in a world where fairies, mermaids, sirens, bards, wolves, and a phoenix were a daily part of my life. It wasn't so hard to think that a beast like a Rougarou existed. However, I couldn't bring myself to think it was me.

FIFTEEN

THE MOMENT I stepped out of the casino to the waiting limo, I heard Malphas' voice in my head.

"*Are you okay?*" he asked.

"*I'm fine.*"

"*Nice collar.*"

"*Yeah, where is Sully?*"

"*Grace ordered him to stay with Tinley and Lyra. When I told him that you said to do it, he didn't believe me. She took care of it.*"

"*Grace.*"

"*She's in Winter right now and can't help us.*"

"*We don't need it. I've got this. Be ready to move when I give the word. Fly your feathered ass back to Dog River and make sure our reinforcements are in place.*"

"*What reinforcements?*"

"*Grace said she was sending reinforcements.*"

"*Oh, yeah, and Lyra shut it down. She's prepared to kill whatever Alpha they bring to her.*"

"*I hope she's ready to face me.*"

"You are the Alpha!"

"Are you flying yet?"

He huffed in my head, but his voice faded. I sat down in the limo next to my mother. She wore a black dress, long and elegant. Various rings adorned her fingers. One of them caught my eye. The horns of a stag twisted in a circle like a crown of thorns.

"Where did you get that one?" I asked when she caught me staring for too long.

She pulled the antlered ring from her finger. "This one was given to me by the Great King Oberon. A token of his appreciation. You see, Son, there was a time when I saw the world as he did, but now, he is dead. I see the world through my own eyes, and I'll make that vision match reality no matter how long it takes."

"And taking over the pure packs helps that effort?"

"You act like you care."

"I do. I'm wolf first."

"That's a shame, because you are much better suited for fairy. You have the fire in your belly and the anger to match. I could use your support. I think the longer that you remain with our organization you will see that we are on the right path," she said.

"What's at the end of that path?" I feared to know, but I needed to know.

"I'm not ready to share that with you. I do not trust you. I would love to trust you. I want us to be a family."

"That's not going to happen," I said.

She slipped the ring back on her finger, and we sat in silence. I watched trees and swamps through the tinted windows. Each mile taking us closer to the Dog River pack. This might be my only chance to squash this, but was I prepared to kill my mother. I remembered how she had destroyed the Whiskey Chito pack. And even though

Frank and Regina weren't my parents, they died because of Araxia's schemes. My real father, that I had met, died by her hand. I could kill her, and I would.

The houses became familiar as we rolled into the little town along the Dog River where Lyra's pack lived. We drove past her aunt's clapboard. I hoped that Tinley was safe within those walls.

"The matriarchs have no real power. They are past shifting age. Besides from what I hear, they believe that you are their savior. When we arrive at the gathering, Rocco will introduce you, then you are to take your new mate. Lyra is a powerful wolf. She will produce a favorable offspring," Mother said.

"She will cut me off before she lets me do that to her," I said.

"I didn't say let. You will take her as I command," she said. I felt the power behind her command. Playing along, I obeyed.

"Yes, Mother," I said.

She hummed. "I love the sound of that. Mother."

"Tell me why," I said as we pulled up outside of Sally's Restaurant. It seemed the whole pack had gathered to see their new Alpha. My stomach churned at what was coming. I needed Lyra to play along, but I knew she wouldn't.

"Did you tell her it was me?"

"She's refused to speak to anyone except Tinley and her aunts. Sully is camped out on their back porch because she said he's not to be allowed inside. Echo is across the way in a tree over the bar."

"Anyone else here?"

"No."

I watched the pack gather around Rocco as he explained what was about to happen. Lyra protested and claimed she'd made a deal with Creed. Rocco shut her down, telling her that she wasn't losing her pack. She would continue to be the female leader, but that she would accept the Alpha that they provided.

"I don't know who you think is in that car, but I'm telling you right now that I'm not going to be any man's incubator!" Lyra shouted.

Aspen stood next to her with Cortland. I didn't see James anywhere, but I hoped he was near. I wanted as many people that were loyal to Lyra as possible to see what was going to happen. Cort coaxed her to calm down, and Aspen got in her face.

"Showtime," my mother said beside me. I wanted to stick my claws through her neck, but I couldn't risk leaving Lyra to Rocco and Creed.

"Members of the Dog River pack, this move to strengthen your future will ensure that your children and their children will be powerful and autonomous. This generation will pay the price, so to speak, to make sure that you and yours have a brighter tomorrow. Our benefactor is not without compassion, so she has allowed us to bring an Alpha to you that we think you will accept as a leader for this pack," Rocco said. He motioned to the car, and the door opened for me.

"Go make Momma proud," Araxia said.

I looked back at her. "The next time I see you will be the last day you draw breath," I said. She cackled as I stepped out of the limo. I straightened the monkey suit they'd put me in, and I hid my stump inside the arm of my jacket.

The members of the pack gasped as I walked toward Rocco. When I dared to look at Lyra, her face shocked me. Instead of anger, I saw relief. She thought she'd handed me off to die. When she realized that they'd turned it around on her, she turned green.

Her pink lips formed the word, "No."

I tore my eyes away from her, stepping up next to Rocco who patted me on the shoulder like we were buds. I wanted to put my claws through his throat, too. A whole new level of throat punch. Werewolf style.

"Most of you know Dominick Meyer. He has come to take the Alpha spot in your pack to make you stronger. He has graciously accepted your female Alpha as his mate." I cleared my throat when he said it, because I hadn't graciously accepted anything. His sideways grin almost made me lose what little composure that I held. "Would you like to say a few words, Alpha Meyer?"

The blood in my veins vibrated with the power of an Alpha. Being addressed as such made my body rattle. Rocco had endowed me with power. People in the pack were already accepting me, and I felt it. This was not what I wanted to happen.

"I have nothing to say other than I made an oath to Lyra to protect the Dog River pack for as long as it needed me," I said, which was the complete truth.

"Wonderful. Now, Miss Rochon, if you would join us," Rocco said, beckoning her toward us with his fingers. She shook her head, and he showed her his fangs. She showed hers back, but Aspen and Cort pleaded with her to not make a scene. She reluctantly walked forward to stand with us. "Yes, they make a wonderful couple."

Whenever Lyra was near me, I could feel her power too. The Alpha inside of her spoke to me. Her composure hung by a very, thin thread.

"Now, if the two of you will please join us in the vehicles," Rocco said.

"No," I said.

"No? I don't think you are in any position to tell me what to do," he said back with a sneer.

125

"You just made me the Alpha of this pack, and I'm telling you 'no.'"

"Well, there's a matter of baby making..."

"That is not going to happen!" Lyra shouted. Goddess help me, I stepped in front of her.

"It's not going to happen on ground that is owned by our pack," I said. "If we are to build the future of these wolves, we are going to do it on our own turf."

Rocco looked at me, then back to the car where my mother sat behind the darkened windows. Rocco sighed and I knew I had won. Mother never ordered me to go back with her. She couldn't do it now without exposing herself to this crowd.

"Very well. We will be back each day to check on your progress," he said. "I hope you can perform."

I wanted to respond like a juvenile, but I kept my mouth shut. Creed walked past me and nudged my shoulder.

"Maybe he's shooting blanks like his *daddy*," Creed said.

I stepped toward him and he flinched. That was all the confirmation that I needed. Creed Martin was afraid of me. And he had every right to be. He was on my list. A list that grew by the moment.

As they walked away, I felt Lyra's tight grip on my arms. The crowd dispersed, leaving me standing with her, Cort, and Aspen.

"What the hell just happened here?" Aspen asked. Lyra seemed to have drifted into shock.

I snapped my fingers in front of her face. She blinked several times, then grabbed my hand. "You aren't dead."

"No, fortunately for me, you sold me to a man that hates my guts, but is controlled by my mother," I said.

"The fairy?"

"She was in the car I got out of," I said. She reached up and touched the collar.

"She's controlling you," Lyra said.

"She *thinks* she is controlling me."

"I can feel the power in that thing over here. She's controlling you," Apsen said.

"How can we know for sure?" Cort asked.

"Because I have no intention on fucking a backstabber," I said, walking away from them toward Malphas who had shifted to human and stood under a tree like a goth druid in a dark cloak. "What's with the robe?"

"My other items were dirty and the laundry at the hotel was broken," he said.

"Nice. You look like a random NPC. Give me my next quest," I said.

"I'll open my robe and sell you some potions," he replied.

"Whoa! Too much, Raven. Too much," I said.

"Why? We are practically intimate as it is," Malphas replied.

"There you go making it even weirder," I said.

"It isn't unusual for fairies to have multiple partners," he said.

"That's not what I meant. Damn it. I'm a wolf. Not a fairy," I protested. "I need a fucking cuff."

"Would you like to purchase one?" He opened his cloak, and I jumped back hiding my eyes. He laughed. Echo laughed in my head. Cort and Aspen laughed behind me. When I summoned enough courage to look at him, he was fully clothed under the cloak. A single leather cuff hung from the inside.

"Grace," I said.

"She thinks of everything," he replied.

"How did she get it here so quickly?" I asked.

"Air mail," a young female voice said behind me. I spun around to see Wynonna Riggs, the Phoenix, leaning on a motorcycle next to her boyfriend, Kyrie Babineau.

"Damn. I told you not to come here, but it's so good to see you," I said, rushing over to hug her. She felt so warm, and I didn't realize how much I had missed her. I shook Kyrie's hand. "It's okay to see you, too."

"Just okay? Come on, Nick. Give me a little something," Kyrie protested. He was rarely serious. Wynonna was overly serious. They kinda matched. I patted him on the shoulder. Everyone had moved over to where I'd greeted Winnie and Kyrie, except Lyra. She stood muttering near the tree. Malphas handed me the cuff, and I put it on feeling the power rush through me.

"Nice collar," Winnie said.

"Yeah, now your mother owns me more than ever," I said.

"She's always owned you," Winnie teased.

"That's true, too," I admitted. "Let me talk to her, then I want to see my brother. We have things to discuss."

I strode back to Lyra who jumped when she realized how close I'd gotten without her noticing. "Are you in on it?" she asked.

"I have a collar on my neck. What do you think? Do you think I'd put one of these on willingly?" I asked.

"Your fairy queen owns you," she growled.

"No. I already have a blood oath to Grace and Levi. This was protection from my own mother. This was protection for you to make sure I wasn't forced to do something neither of us wanted."

"You've got that right, and if you think for one second..." I stepped into her personal space, cutting her off.

"I didn't want to do this, but you leave me no choice.

Lyra Rochon, you are a bitch. You have got to calm the fuck down and realize that I'm here to help you. Even though you sold me out, I'm still here to help your pack. I made an oath that I intend to keep, and I suggest you get with the program or get the fuck out of the way. Are we clear?"

Her mouth moved, but no sound came out. I knew that every time I tried to Alpha her; she would get aroused. It didn't matter if she did. I wouldn't touch her. Not ever again. My feelings still swirled around, and my heart pounded in my chest, but my willpower held strong.

"Lyra, are we clear?" I asked again.

"You can't take my pack."

"I'm not taking your pack. I'm saving it and you, even though you don't deserve it." I turned on my heel and walked away, leaving her stunned. "Where is Sully?"

"Come on, I'll give you a ride," Kyrie said, motioning to his bike.

"I'd rather shift and run than get on that thing and ride with you," I said. He knew I'd refuse. Malphas pointed to the SUV. We piled in leaving Lyra behind with Cort and Aspen.

"Wow. I didn't think you could find more of a handful than me and Mom," Winnie said as she snuggled next to Kyrie in the back seat.

"Well, I did. It doesn't matter. She turned me over to Creed Martin. It's a betrayal that I will never forgive," I said.

"Forgive her not for her peace, but for your own," Malphas said.

"Forgive her because she was protecting her pack the only way she knew how," Winnie added.

"None of that makes a difference. She knew it was more than just charity for me. I gave her my oath," I said.

Kyrie exhaled heavily, knowing the power of an oath.

"What was it, if not charity?" Winnie asked.

"Wynonna," I grumbled.

"Say it," she pressed.

"It doesn't matter now. I was a fool, but I'll keep my oath. I'll save Dog River even if that means saving her, but she will no longer hold my heart," I said, laying my head back on the rest above the seat.

Malphas pulled up in front of the yellow clapboard house. Sully sat on the porch with Eula, Aggie, and Tinley drinking lemonade. When I stepped out of the SUV, he rushed to me, hugging me tightly.

"I see you were real worried," I said.

"News travels fast, and the ladies wanted to enjoy the cool afternoon on the porch," he said. Then, he cocked his head. "What's wrong?"

"Things happened, and we need to talk. Like right now."

"Is it that serious?" he asked, watching Wynonna and Kyrie climb out of the SUV. "Winnie!" He hugged her and shook hands with Kyrie.

"Lordy mercy, I've never met a Phoenix," Eula called out.

"I'll introduce them. You go," Malphas urged.

I watched Winnie and Kyrie step up on the porch and greet the older ladies. Winnie gravitated toward Tinley which didn't surprise me. In maturity levels, they were about the same. Winnie was infinitely more powerful than Tinley, but that never stopped Winnie from making a new friend.

"What is it?" Sully pressed.

"Not here. We need to get away from all ears," I said.

"Well, let's go for a walk," he suggested.

I nodded and followed him to the back of the house toward the forest. My nerves ramped up and my heart pounded. He continued to walk even though he knew my anxiety had skyrocketed. Once we reached the edge of the swamp he stopped, looking around us. I knew he was checking the surroundings for auras.

"Are we alone?" I asked.

"Except for a few legit critters," he replied, speaking in an overly country accent. His smile faded. "I hear your heart racing. Did you see our mother?"

"I did. She was in the car with me. She's the one that put this collar on me."

"I didn't want to mention it, but I know that Grace broke Mother's hold on you."

"She did, but she told me that we…" My voice cracked like a fifteen-year-old going through puberty. Sully laid his hand on my shoulder.

"Whatever it is, we can handle it," he said.

"We are triplets. Frank couldn't have kids. She broke us up at birth and put me with Whiskey Chito to toughen me up. We aren't half-siblings," I said as my voice choked.

"And I had to go and fucking kiss you," Sully said.

"You did! You moron!" I replied, shaking from the anxiety.

"Is it true?" he asked.

"Fairies can't lie," I said.

"Oh, that's right." Then, he wrapped me up in a huge hug. He nearly crushed me. "It didn't matter if we were half or whole. You have always been my brother."

I stepped back, thankful for his way of putting things into words that I couldn't. "I love you and Suzi. You have been the best family to me. I love my Shady Grove family, but you are my blood."

"Always will be. What else?" he asked.

"This part is going to piss you off. I want you to know

that I beat the crap out of him until Mother put me down using the collar," I said.

"What are you talking about?"

"Michael Handley works for Araxia," I said.

"Oh, fuck no! I'm going to Shady Grove," he said, stomping back toward the house.

"Sully! No, you can't. Grace knows. Callum knows. They are playing him to get information." Sully stopped and put his hands on his hips. "You can't deny how much you care about him."

"I never had to deny it, Nick! I didn't have to admit it either. I'm going to rip his head off. I bet they didn't know in the beginning. I need to call him. It's too dangerous for him to keep this up. That means that Mother knows who he is. She knows he is the last Native American white wolf. She probably wants him for some of her crazy wolf breeding shit."

"Wolf breeding shit?"

"She's always had interest in the bloodlines of wolves. She told me she was trying to make a wolf like a Rougarou. That's why she was in Houma. No one knows more about the Rougarou than my old pack. She probably thinks he has to be part of the bloodline. She isn't watching Shady Grove. She's watching Callum."

My face fell. "Tinley."

"What?" he asked.

I sprinted back to the house with Sully on my heels. Lyra had arrived and she sat on the porch with everyone else. She refused to look at me which was all the better.

"We need to go inside now," I said.

"You don't order us around!" Lyra protested.

"Shut-up!" Eula and Aggie yelled at her.

"Please. I need all of us inside right now," I said.

"You heard the Alpha. Everyone inside."

It was a full production to get everyone inside including the precious lemonade pitcher and glasses. Once Eula and Aggie were settled on their couch, we gathered to talk within the safeties of their Wiccan ward.

"What is Tinley?" I asked. Tinley whimpered and hid her face behind Lyra.

"You have no right," Lyra protested.

"I mean it, Lyra! I swear to all that is good and holy, if you don't stop bitch blocking me, I am going to..." I grunted realizing that I couldn't beat the shit out of her. It wasn't right.

"Lyra, as the matriarch of this pack, I'm ordering you to cut this shit out," Eula said. "He has done nothing to harm any of us while you sold him out. It was a bad deal, and you know it was. You should apologize to him, but I don't think that is going to help."

"It won't," I said. Lyra didn't speak again. "Now. What is she?"

"She is the last of her kind," Aggie said.

"I'm willing to bet she isn't," I said with a smile. Tinley tilted her head to the side, waiting for my explanation.

SIXTEEN

DUSK GREETED us with the sounds of the bayou as we got in the SUV to leave. Tinley was exactly what I had expected. Now that I knew one of my mother's goals, I had an advantage to catch her. I was going to need help.

Lyra didn't speak for the rest of the night while we discussed plans to protect the pack. Winnie and Kyrie had to run an errand for me back in Steelshore, so we dropped them off at their motorcycles.

"Be careful on that thing," I said, hugging her.

"I will. You are like some sort of overbearing uncle," she smirked.

"I *am* Levi's brother," I smirked back.

"That is so fake," she said, then snapped on her helmet. I looked at Kyrie who nodded.

"I know. Don't hurt her. Look out for her. Yadda, yadda," he said.

"I know you will," I said.

"Oh really?" he replied.

"Yes." He grinned, then fired up the hog. We waved as they stirred up dust, riding out of town.

After they were gone, I looked at Sully, Malphas, and Echo. "We have plans to make," I said.

"Let's do it," Malphas replied.

"I need a good fight to work out my aggression," Sully said.

"Yeah, that's not what you need," I teased.

"That, too," he replied.

The four of us made plans well into the night as the full moon rose above the Dog River Hotel. Sully and I made a phone call to Suzi giving her the good news. She was thrilled to find out that our sibling status had changed. I couldn't ask for a better family. Well, maybe a better mother.

"One day, I want you to tell me more about Hiram," I told Sully as we laid down to rest.

"He was hard on the outside, but he loved us. He was the reason I fought who I was for so long. I didn't want to let him down. He put pressure on me, but never more than what a normal, loving parent does to protect their children. I just wish I could have helped him," Sully said.

"I should have been there," I said.

"You were in Shady Grove where you needed to be."

"Now I need to be here."

"What are you going to do about her?" I knew he mean Lyra.

"Hell, if I know. If she would just crack that shell of hers just a little bit."

"People build walls over time. You can't expect to break them down overnight or with a couple of fucks."

'Oh, thank you, wise one." He laughed in the darkness. "I meant what I said though. There is no us for she and I anymore."

"On one hand, I see what you are saying. She betrayed you. Like Judas-level betrayal. But I know that if you still love her, love will win in the end."

"You and your rosy outlooks." Sully had always been positive. My mother called it a weakness. I considered it a talent. He had plenty to be negative about, but he never let it get to him. And now that we knew Callum wasn't so involved. I dared to hope for a happy ending for them.

I woke up in the clothes I'd worn yesterday. At least, I'd removed the coat of the fancy suit. Someone banged on the door.

"I'm coming!" I shouted.

"Phrasing," Sully said.

"Heh," I replied and opened the door. A steaming cup of coffee was shoved into my face.

"I brought one for Sully, too," Lyra said.

"Is it laced with arsenic?" Sully asked. I waited for her to blow up, but she just giggled. Straight up, giggled. I sighed. My brother had all the charm.

"No, arsenic. I'd find more delightful and painful ways to kill you if I wanted," Lyra returned.

"Would you like to come in?" I asked.

"Actually, I'd like to talk. Just us," she said.

Sully climbed out of the bed in his birthday suit and took the cup from Lyra.

"No shame," I muttered.

"Too bad he's gay," Lyra said.

"Oh, good grief," I said, stepping outside and shutting the door on my snickering brother.

"No need to worry. You look better naked than he does," Lyra said. I spat coffee. She giggled again.

"What's with the giggling?" I had to ask.

"Well, I'm working up to saying something that I don't normally say, and I'm nervous," she said. She walked away from the hotel toward a small bench that sat near the road under a tree. She sat down, and I joined her. "Did you sleep in your clothes?"

"Yeah, fell asleep making plans," I said.

"For the pack?"

"Yes," I replied.

"I know that you are helping. I know that you care about what happens here. But I need to know if it was because of your mother or if it was for me?" she asked.

"Now, it's because I made an oath, and I intend to keep it."

"I get that. But before, when you came," she said.

"You know the answer to that," I replied.

"I need to hear you say it."

"Why? It doesn't matter now."

"It may not for you, but it does for me."

"Lyra, I came here for you. Because *you* asked me. I knew what you were up against, and I didn't want to see you face it alone when I could stand by you. And I will stand by you against Rocco, Creed, and my mother."

"And then you will leave," she said.

"I don't think I'll be able to leave. Not anytime soon. I'm not going to assume that we can beat them, so I'm certainly not counting on killing them. And unless they are dead, Tinley and the pack will never be safe," I said.

"I'm sorry."

The apology hung between us. Not a single bone in my body wanted me to accept it. I knew she was sorry the moment I'd opened the door, but that didn't change the fact that I couldn't trust her. Packs were built on trust. I saw in her what her pack saw. She was the reason they wouldn't support her. It wasn't her fault that she didn't know how to lead. Some are naturals like Sully. Some were too forceful, and brutes like me. Lyra just didn't trust anyone. Ever.

"What made you distrust me?"

"I apologized," she whined.

"I need more than that if we are going to work together. Work. And I mean that. Nothing more. Not ever."

"I get that. Okay." She started to huff but held it back.

"I've just been so afraid for Tinley. I hope what you said is true. I want to see it for myself before I can believe it. Between protecting her legacy and protecting the pack, I became overwhelmed. And I certainly never expected to be so intrigued with a lone wolf that happened into my space." Suddenly, I remembered what my mother had told me about the night I met Lyra.

"That wasn't by accident."

"Huh?"

"Mother was there that night in disguise. Do you remember anyone urging you to talk to me?"

She thought for a moment. "Yeah! There was this beautiful blonde sitting next to me. Men kept asking her to dance, but she kept turning them down. We began to trade small talk, but when I saw you come in, she noticed. She immediately started pushing me toward you."

"My mother wanted me here for this takeover . I'm sure she had planned it long before she pushed us together. But you should know that she influenced you that night."

"Influenced? Like a spell?"

"I don't know if she used a spell or not. She didn't say she did. But I thought you should know."

"She didn't influence me the second time."

"No, you didn't need to be influenced. The wolves inside of us were drawn to each other's power."

She closed her eyes, knowing what I was saying was the truth.

"She knew I'd come to you for help and drag you into this."

"It was exactly what she wanted."

"Is that how you see our relationship? As something that she forced us into?"

"No. My feelings were real."

"Were?"

"Were."

She bit her lip to keep it from trembling. "I know I fucked up. I promise not to fight you anymore. You have control of all of it. You can even be the Alpha."

I took her hand, because I couldn't resist it. Fucking tears were brutal on a male psyche. "I don't want Alpha. I want you to be the strongest and best Alpha for your pack. I'm just here to help you. Will you just let me help? Will you stop fighting me at every move?"

She nodded her head as the tears fell. "Yes." I'd never heard her voice so light and without power. I'd broken her down. I could have easily taken the pack from her. She realized that now, but she also knew that I would never do that to her. Today would start the rebuilding of Lyra Rochon. I couldn't do it for her, but I'd be here to advise and help.

But no apology would ever make up for her betrayal. Perhaps we could make a tenuous friendship out of it, but it would take me a very, long time to ever trust her again.

SEVENTEEN

AGGIE SAT a plate full of biscuits and gravy in front of me. It reminded me of The Grove diner in Shady Grove. Luther Harris made the best food. This looked just as good.

"Thank you, Aggie," I said.

The Aunts insisted that Sully and I move into the house with them. Apparently, the place was a lot larger on the inside than we thought. Very few houses in this area had full basements because of the potential for flooding, but this place had a whole other living space which meant I didn't have to room with my brother. We'd been here two days.

Each day, Rocco and Creed would come to check on Lyra and me. We played the happy couple with her allowing me to lead. Behind the scenes, we were setting up a plan to separate the pack from Araxia and her goons.

Sully had called Callum several times, but the calls went unanswered. I assured him that he needed to give it time, but my brother had been searching for something his whole life. Now that he had it in his sights, he didn't want to let it go.

Lyra had done as I'd asked. She didn't fight me at every suggestion. She even helped us with getting Willow to set up small wards on several main houses in town for the pack to retreat and hide, if needed.

Sully and I had trained some of the bigger guys and the women that wanted to join to fight. James McCaffrey had helped us with that. He had military experience and had done some MMA fighting. We continued the ruse for the whole pack, but James knew that Lyra and I weren't really together.

We walked around town with small public displays of affection. Those were the worst for me. I played the part, but Lyra still felt it. I couldn't fathom why she thought I'd ever get over being sold instead of being trusted. It was something I could not forgive. She never complained.

Sully asked me if I thought I'd ever forgive her, and the answer in my gut was always no. He never gave his opinion on the topic.

Suzi and Reuben were coming to visit. It seemed only natural that my sister would come to wish me well with my new relationship. I looked forward to seeing her. She said she had a surprise for me. She would be here tomorrow.

Winnie had contacted the friend I needed to see. He didn't want to come into town, so Lyra and I were going to motorcycle north to a small café where I'd first met Seamus Daragh, the vampirate.

"Ready to go?" I asked her as she exited the house in tight blue jeans and a Metallica t-shirt.

"Who's driving?" she asked.

"Whatever. I always drive," I replied. We could joke, but sometimes it felt fake. Forced.

"I'll hold on for dear life," she said, climbing on the motorcycle behind me.

"Good idea." I snapped on my helmet and revved the engine.

She wrapped her arms around me, and we raced toward Steelshore. We knew Creed and Rocco would arrive in the evening, and we had to be back, or there would be hell to pay.

Seamus was already inside, when we arrived. Lyra sat down in the booth, and I sat next to her. Seamus lifted his eyebrow at me.

"So, this is the infamous, Lyra Rochon," Seamus said, reaching across the table to take her hand. He watched me but spoke to her. "It is my extreme pleasure to meet you."

"Perhaps it could be mine," Lyra replied. Seamus was a charmer, and she picked up on it.

"I think the Alpha would remove my throat," he said.

"Probably not," Lyra said, pulling her hand from his grasp.

"Oh, well, that's a shame. Now, what can I do for you, Mr. Meyer?" Seamus asked.

"You were in Vegas when you met Grace and Levi," I said.

"Yes, Grace makes an impression on a man, as you know," he replied.

"Yes, she does. They were there to get information on her mother who was involved with the trafficking." He leaned back in his seat. I watched as he assessed the situation. The vampirate was the ultimate smooth operator. He claimed not to have a side in the fight, but he'd clearly been on ours since he'd met Grace. He'd taken a particular interest in Wynonna, which is why I called him when I left Steelshore for Dog River. I knew he would keep an unbiased eye on her. It wasn't that I didn't trust her abilities. I didn't trust her judgment when it came to Kyrie Babineau.

He'd proven himself to her, and I respected that, but he hadn't proven shit to me. Not to the level that I'd trust him with the whole operation in Steelshore.

"Have you ever met her mother?" I asked.

"I have not," Seamus replied.

"There are three witches involved with this. Fairy witches. I cannot figure out their place in it all. How many witches are there in the Order of the Red Cloak?" I asked, knowing that Seamus had traveled this world. He'd seen a lot of things in his days as a pirate, and even more as a dark room-dealing vampire.

"I know of them. Thankfully, I never crossed the path of one. There are always three. If those perish, three more rise up to take their place. One of their principles is that they choose their successor the moment they become part of the order. Always female. Always powerful. The power from each passes to the next to join their already existing powers," he explained.

"Does that mean that the current witches knew the dead ones?" Lyra asked.

"Not necessarily."

"How is that possible?"

"The heirs are chosen by magic. It's a ritual," he said.

I looked around the café and realized that no one had come to take our order. "What did you do?" I asked, remembering the last time I saw him here.

He shrugged. "I did the only thing I could possibly do."

"Which was what?" Lyra asked.

"I touched them all," he said, narrowing his eyes at her hand where he had touched her. He cut his eyes to me. It surprised me that part of me didn't want him to show her. "No protest?" he asked.

"None," I replied.

"What does he do?" Lyra asked.

The moans from the kitchen started, and Lyra looked alarmed. Seamus grinned like a Cheshire cat.

"That. He does that," I said, shaking my head.

"What? It's a perfectly harmless tool that I use to distract a human from a supernatural discussion," he said as one of the women in the back started screaming, "Yes! Yes!"

"Wow," Lyra said and looked down at her hand.

"Want a taste?" he asked.

"No, thank you," she replied, tucking her hand under the table.

"He's already touched you. He could do it if he wanted," I said.

"No means no," she said.

"Ah! Yes. Consent is necessary."

"Do you ask permission when you do it to them?" I asked.

"Not so much, but they can choose to fight the feeling as it begins. Most do not. Those that do are truly strong individuals," he said.

"Did you touch Wynonna?" I asked.

He grinned. "I've touched Wynonna multiple times. I would never harm her."

"She fought it?" I asked.

"She practically ignored it," he replied. "A rare beast. I'd heard that you couldn't seduce a Phoenix, but I wondered if it applied to just the men."

"Sexist bastard," Lyra muttered.

"Ah, yes. I can be, but it was more of a science experiment," he said.

"Grace would dust you," I reminded him.

He laughed. "I suppose so, but I did it anyway."

"Keep your hands off her," I said.

"First of all, one thing you need to understand is that Wynonna Riggs is a strong young woman. Secondly, she doesn't need your protection or mine. Thirdly, I consider her to be the best of all of you. An innocent soul given an enormous gift. It's about time you all gave her the respect she deserves," Seamus said with a passionate diatribe.

"Sounds like the vampirate has a crush on your Phoenix," Lyra said.

"It is not a crush. It is an admiration for a truly magnificent creature," Seamus said.

He did respect her, but I think Lyra hit on something I hadn't noticed. Seamus did treat her differently than any of us. I made a note in my head to warn Winnie. Or perhaps she didn't need warning. Perhaps I needed to trust her instinct, but it didn't mean I wouldn't keep an eye on the situation.

"Back to the witches. Is there any way for me to track them? Is it possible that Grace's mother is now one of the Order? I recently saw my mother. I didn't get the impression that she was dabbling in a form of fairy witch magic," I said.

"You wouldn't see it. How many years did witches walk in Shady Grove with no one knowing? What was the Druid's daughter's name?" he asked.

"Kady," I said.

"Yes, that one."

"But if what you said was true, more than likely she wasn't always one of the witches. But she was an heir."

"Yes, but she would have had powers that she kept hidden. I would suggest that you check for them in your pack. They would be able to mask their magic. If they are involved, I bet one of them is inside already," Seamus said.

"Any suggestions on how to find them?" I asked.

The last of the moans subsided in the kitchen. They were replaced with snores.

"Good sex wears you out." He grinned with pleasure as though he had accomplished something himself. I rolled my eyes. "I've always steered clear of the Order. I know you can't in this case, but I don't have all the answers for you."

"Thank you for what information you have provided. What is the cost?" I asked.

"You offend me, Dominick Meyer." He rose from the table and straightened the coat of his suit. His skull topped cane appeared at his side. The cane had magical protections built into it. It made him immune to most magic.

"Thank you," Lyra repeated my gratitude.

"You let me know if you change your mind," he said, giving her a sly wink, then walked out of the café.

A waitress approached us while trying to tuck her hair into place. "Can I get you a cup of coffee or something to eat?"

"I'd like a cup of coffee. What about you?" I asked Lyra.

"Yes, please," she replied. The waitress walked away still managing her wild sex hair. I wondered if Seamus' touch resulted in some sort of mutual gratification with whoever else had been in the kitchen. "You weren't going to stop him from doing that to me?"

"Why would I? It's your life. Your choice."

The waitress returned with two cups and poured coffee in each. She dropped packets of sugar and small creamers on the table, then hurried away.

"I guess I hoped there might be something left." She caught herself saying the words. I hated when she mentioned us as a couple. She changed her approach. "Thank you for everything you've done for the pack.

Thank you for pretending for my sake. I fucked up, and I know it."

I took slow sips of the coffee. I knew she meant it, but I wasn't swayed in the least. "I made an oath."

"It's more than an oath. You care about stopping your mother. This is bigger than just Dog River. This goes to why she was watching Callum. Why she might go after Tinley. You want to stop her, and I promise to help you do it. Why did you ask about Grace's mother? I haven't heard that come up."

It was just like Lyra to change the subject when she knew I wasn't going to budge.

"I think maybe that Grace's mother and my mother are in on this together. There are three witches. There has to be one more," I said.

"Do you think it's someone you know?" she asked.

"Unlikely, but if what Seamus said is true. We can't just kill them to stop it. Three more will rise up. We have to stop the cycle," I said.

Lyra sipped on the cup of coffee and stared out the window. "We should get back."

"Yes, we need to pretend for Rocco and Creed."

"I think they know. They are just waiting for a way to prove it," she said.

"Perhaps, but let them come. We are ready for them."

We left a generous tip for the waitress who had to "endure" Seamus' touch, then rode back to Dog River. When we arrived, the Martins were waiting on us. I pretended not to notice them sitting at Sally's Restaurant as I helped Lyra off the motorcycle.

I cupped her cheek with my hand. "They are here," I whispered, knowing that the wolves might be listening.

"Yes," she replied. Consent. I kissed her slowly as if I'd

never kissed her before. She wobbled when I let her go. "Holy shit, Nick."

"What?" I asked.

"What was that?"

"A kiss," I replied. Her reaction confused me. We'd played this game many times for the Martins.

"It felt different."

I took several deep breaths, listening to her heartbeat. It hadn't felt any different for me, but she clearly had been affected. She planted kisses on my neck and a small moan escaped her lips.

"Fucking Seamus," I muttered. "He did this to you."

"It feels like you," Lyra moaned. I looked at the Martins who were approaching and I didn't know what to do about my love drunk fake girlfriend who now had her hands under my shirt.

"Lyra," I hissed. She ignored me.

"Well, this is an interesting development," Creed said.

"Looks like they are *really* together, doesn't it?" Rocco asked. Perhaps Seamus had done me a favor. We weren't fooling anyone. Not really.

"We've been together." I grabbed Lyra's chin, tilting her head up to me. "Stop, Little Wolf. Save it for later." Lyra shook with sexual tension.

"I'd like to watch them fuck," Rocco said. "In fact, I'm going to ask Araxia if I can."

"Araxia doesn't decide whether or not you enter my bedroom. I assure you that you will never watch a damn thing," I snarled. Lyra dropped to her knees in front of me, bowing her head. I ignored it.

"Wow! Would you look at that? He's fucking tamed her!" Rocco said.

It didn't matter that Lyra and I weren't really together. It pissed me off that this sorry excuse for a man would make that assumption about a beautiful woman. My claws stretched out of my hands and my fangs extended.

Rocco took a step back.

"What the fuck are you?" Creed asked while pulling Rocco away.

Looking down at my hands, I couldn't believe what I was seeing. Claws twice as long as they normally were curled out of my paws. I felt my fangs brushing my lower jaw. Black hairs jutted out of my sleeves, and my feet hurt inside my shoes.

"I'm telling you to leave my territory. If you so much as look at this pack again," I popped my claws in and out for effect, "I will slice you open. Now apologize to Lyra for being rude."

"I ain't apologizing for nothing," Rocco said, as his father dragged him away from me.

"I'll make you," I said, stepping toward them. My shoes ripped open and long hairy feet jutted out of the torn soles. Long claws extended from them. I looked up to find the moon, but a bank of clouds obscured it. My internal mind panicked, while my outward body advanced on the Martins.

I grabbed Rocco by the neck. Creed ran to his car and sped off, leaving his crying son behind. I threw him down next to Lyra. I felt possessed. I was doing what I wanted to do, instead of suppressing my anger and hatred for this piece of shit.

"Now! Fucking apologize!" I demanded.

"I..I..I'm..I'm so sorry," he stammered.

"Now, I kill you," I said, stepping toward him.

"Dominick!" a female voice cried out. "Stop!"

Rocco scooted away from me along the gravel. "I'm sorry. I said I was sorry," he pleaded.

"Yes, and I'll make it quick instead of drawing it out. I

owe you this for other things," I said. Raising my claws, I stopped hearing another voice calling out to me.

Spinning around, I saw Sully standing next to my very pregnant sister, Suzi.

"You gotta stop, Nick," Suzi pleaded.

"He's going to die," I snarled. Something inside of me fought for control. I couldn't subdue the beast that had emerged. Turning back to the downed Rocco, a white wolf stood in my path. Its bright blue eyes flickered as it growled.

"Move!" I demanded. It didn't move. In fact, it burrowed down waiting for me to make a move.

Lyra looked up at me in shock. "Please don't hurt her," she said with tears, running down her cheeks.

I stumbled backward away from them. The claws retracted, and I returned to my normal human body. My head swirled, and I staggered into the street. Sully ran to me and caught me before I hit the pavement.

"Are you okay? Talk to me," he pleaded.

"What was that?" I said, trying to catch my breath.

"Rougarou," he replied.

EIGHTEEN

JUST WHEN I thought I had some semblance of control; my body had decided to hulk out. For the life of me, I couldn't place what had triggered the transformation. Even as I slept, my mind played through dozens of scenarios about how I had reacted to the Martins. What was different? What caused the beast inside to make an appearance? I didn't feel any more angry than normally.

I listed them in my mind. Lyra was under Seamus' touch spell, that somehow, he had diverted to make me the focus of it. Lyra, even with the change in her attitude, would have never knelt before me. She didn't have a submissive bone in her body.

The Martins had pissed me off, which wasn't a new thing. I had remembered looking to the sky, but only seeing clouds. Was it a full moon? I wasn't sure.

My head pounded as I looked at Rocco Martin cowering before me in my dream. I swiped my claws at him spraying his blood all over me and onto the black pavement. The Rougarou loved the blood and reveled in the death.

Jolting up in the bed, I screamed, but I couldn't tell if that part was in my dream or had I actually screamed at a nightmare like a little girl.

Lyra sat on the edge of the bed holding a damp bath cloth. Her eyes widened, and she backed away.

"I'm me. It's me," I muttered, trying to fight back the dream.

"You've been feverish," she said, keeping her distance.

"Did I kill him? My memory is jumbled."

"You remember transforming?" she asked.

"Yes, but I don't know why."

Sully stepped into the room and leaned against the door. "I made some calls to some of the Houma pack that remains. I got nothing on a Rougarou that was anything other than legend."

"If I am this, shouldn't you be this, too?" I asked. He pushed off the door and sat down on the bed. Lyra moved toward the door. "Lyra, are you okay? Is Tinley okay?"

"Yes, you didn't harm either of us. I'd once heard that if you knelt before a Rougarou that it wouldn't harm you. When I saw your eyes turn red, I hit my knees hoping it wasn't a tale of some sort," she explained.

"Seamus did something," I said.

"I felt that too, but I fought it," she said.

"You beat it?"

"I think," she said, then left me alone with my brother.

"Suzi. She's pregnant," I said.

"It's interesting that you remember that part. Tell me what all you remember," Sully said.

I told him about going to see Seamus and what he had done to the people at the café and to Lyra. He nodded his head as I went through each part of the confrontation until I blacked out.

"You were there when it went dark," I said.

"You remember all of it. Rocco shifted and ran into the swamps. We tried following him, but we lost him. You didn't kill him. Why did you think you did?"

"In my dreams, I slashed his throat with those claws. It didn't feel real. It was as if something had taken over not just my body, but my mind. I had no control. We have to know what triggered it. I can't protect this pack when I have that beast inside of me," I said.

"You've had that beast inside of you all along. It's not a sudden thing, Nick. It had to be there. But yes, we need to figure it out. The Aunts want to speak to you, but you know they won't come down the stairs," he said.

Only then did I realize I was in the bed that the matriarchs had given me. I raised up and felt like I'd battled the flu. Everything ached. I groaned as I tried to get out of the bed.

"Maybe you should stay and rest," he said.

"No, they will be coming. We have to figure this out now, but maybe you could help me to the shower," I said.

"Sure," he said as he helped me to my feet. I leaned on him feeling the strength of my brother. My mother had said he was weak, but I knew Sully's power wasn't in brutality. He had an uncanny ability to get along with everyone. He was a natural and charismatic leader. I needed him to teach me how to do it. Otherwise, I was going to fail Dog River. As I peeled off my clothes which felt like they had been glued to me, he picked them up one by one and tossed them in the hamper. "When you get out, you need to call Mark."

"Mark? What's wrong with Mark?" I asked.

"He needs to talk to you. He called while you were sleeping," he said.

Mark was my Alpha in Shady Grove. I realized now that the bond between us had snapped. He must have felt it, too. I had accepted the Alpha in me. That was what had triggered the beast. Sully left me, and I stood under the hot water pouring over my aching body. The blood pounding through my veins sang with the power that I had suppressed. This had been lurking beneath the surface for so long, and because of my rejection of an Alpha life, it remained hidden.

An Alpha's first job was to protect his pack. The Martins had insulted Lyra when I thought she had been under Seamus' spell. The instinct to protect her ignited that feeling that I'd denied. Not specifically to Lyra, but to a pack. A family. A home. The longer I stayed in Dog River, the more I felt like I'd found where I was supposed to be. Over the course of a few weeks, the pack had strengthened under my guidance. I was doing something right, but why did the beast feel so wrong? So dark and uncontrollable.

I forced myself to get out of the shower and face the rest of the household, but I called Mark before I went upstairs.

"Hello," he answered, sounding more like a man than the boy he was not so long ago.

"Hey, Mark," I said.

"Just tell me you are okay."

"I'm not sure, but I'll figure it out. What did Sully tell you?"

"He told me everything because I was your Alpha. You were my second-in-command," he said.

"I'm sorry. I don't think I did it consciously. You know that I am just a call away. The Shady Grove pack will always be a part of me. A part of my family."

"But the family is bigger now."

"Yes."

"I felt the connection snap, and honestly, I had expected it a long time ago. I can't thank you enough for your loyalty. I have plenty of candidates here for a new Beta. But you are right, we are family. I just wish you would have called me when you realized what you were facing there."

I knew I hadn't called him because Lyra didn't want it. If I was truly the Alpha now, I needed to respect her desires for the pack. It was still hers. I didn't know how it would work, but we needed to lead together.

"I deferred to Lyra on that decision. I promise to call if I need you," I said.

"What about the beast?" he asked.

"I don't know. If anyone up there has any information about it, I'd be glad to hear it, even if it is a tale or rumor."

"Sure thing. I'll ask around. And I know that I'm less experienced and younger than you, but I am proud to have called you my Beta, but I'm even more proud to call you an Alpha friend."

I chuckled at his maturity. I remembered the love-struck boy following around a pretty little girl. They both had grown up and apart, but their souls were still connected. It would be the same for me. I grew up, too. In letting go of my past. I'd be more willing to embrace the future if I knew what the hell had happened.

"Same, my Brother. Same."

He disconnected the call, and I climbed the stairs to face the matriarchs of the pack I'd claimed. I wondered what they thought of me now. The ladies sat in the living room, sipping tea from antique cups. No one in the room looked at me when I entered, except for Tinley.

"Hi," she said.

KIMBRA SWAIN

I crossed the room and squatted in front of her. "I would never hurt you," I said.

"I wasn't afraid of you. I knew if you killed him that you'd hate yourself for it if you did," she said.

"Thank you," I said, lowering my head.

"You looked awesome," she said. I huffed out a sigh.

I looked up to meet the admiring eyes of the matriarchs. My pregnant sister appeared at the kitchen door. I jumped up and hugged her, placing my hand over her growing belly.

"Wow!"

"You are going to be an uncle," she said.

"I see that. It's amazing," I said, leaning over to kiss her belly.

My heart ached knowing that I didn't have a grasp on the creature inside of me. I could shift at any moment and tear them all apart. Suzi touched my cheek, and I looked at her.

"You would never do anything to hurt your family. Don't worry," she said.

"Where is Reuben?" I asked.

"He went with Aspen, Cort, and James to set up sentries along the main roads. We will be alerted if anyone moves through by car," she said.

"I'm more worried about them coming on all fours," I said.

"Come sit with us," Aggie prodded.

I obeyed and sat across from them. Tinley poured a cup of hot tea for me. I wasn't a fan of hot tea, but I didn't want to be rude.

"Drink the tea, so that I may read the leaves," Eula said.

"You read tea leaves?" I asked.

"Isn't that what I just said?" Eula asked.

I nodded, then sipped the tea slowly. Its bitterness

struck my tongue, and I forced myself to swallow the hot liquid. I finished it quickly then handed the cup to Eula. She refused it.

"Swirl the cup around three times, left to right. Then, slowly tip the cup allowing the remaining liquid to flow out and hit the ground. We will clean it up afterward." I did as she instructed, then she reached for the cup. Tinley got up and cleaned the tea off the floor.

"I would have gotten that," I said. She winked, then disappeared into the kitchen.

"Dominick, focus on your goals. Focus on your distant future."

"Your endgame," Lyra said behind me. It was the first time she had spoken since I'd appeared.

I closed my eyes focusing on the distant future. I saw a family and a pack. That future included my brother happily settled and my sister with lots of kids. I stood in a neighborhood with kids running around my feet and a woman in the distance. I couldn't see her face, but she was there. Someone to share this future with me.

"Your story told by the leaves starts at the top of the cup, being the near future, and the bottom of the cup is the distant future. Around the rim, I see indication of great changes in your life. I see strife, but I also see support and growth. Just below the rim, I see the symbol for a new beginning beside that is a heart."

"What does the heart mean?"

Her eyes twinkled. "Love, of course."

"Oh," I replied.

"Deeper in the cup, I see more discord, but your essence is strong, and you persevere. There are many around you, but you will always carry a solo burden."

"The burden of this transformation?" I asked.

"There is no way to know. The tea leaves are general, not

specific. I suppose that some might see that as a weakness of reading leaves, but I see it as a strength. I can see what is going to happen, but the specifics will ultimately be up to you. You control your destiny," Eula said.

"So much fighting," I muttered.

"You were given this life because you are strong enough to live it," Aggie said. "Even if you don't believe it yet. I do."

"So, do I," Tinley added.

"We all do," Lyra said.

I hoped they were right. I felt the beast inside of me. The desire to rip bodies to shreds lurked just below the surface, and I felt that burning urge.

"What do you know about the Rougarou?" I asked the matriarchs.

"I've never seen one, but there are a lot of stories. I knew they existed. Many say they are cursed by a witch. Some say they are Faeborn wolves that have lost their minds, but clearly you are not mad," Aggie said.

"I feel it crawling under my skin. I'm afraid that it will slaughter you," I admitted.

"First of all, that won't happen here," Eula said and pointed at the rug on the floor. Tinley bent down and rolled it back out of the way. A white hexagon had been drawn in chalk. "One of Willow's protections. She said it was for the wolfman that was to come."

"We are all wolves," I said.

"But you are the only one of us who can walk as a man, but look like a wolf," Aggie said.

"Willow knows about the Rougarou?" I asked.

"It's not like she will give you a straight answer," Lyra offered.

I knew that was true. The witch spoke in riddles. Then,

it occurred to me that she has spoken of the illusion and I just assumed she meant my hand. Maybe she had meant the anger and beast I had repressed. The illusion that everything was alright under the surface.

"The only way you survive this is if you drop the illusion and be truthful to those around you."

"What is it?" Sully asked.

"Willow. She said the only way I survive this is if I drop the illusion. She wasn't talking about my hand. She was talking about the Rougarou. If I can control it, then it will be enough to push back against the takeover," I said.

"But can you control it?" Sully asked.

"I have to believe that I can," I said.

"You can," Tinley said. "If you don't, we will be here to bring you back."

"You need to stay put in this house. Is Callum on the way?" I asked.

"He finally called me back, and yes, I expect him soon," Sully said.

"How are we going to know if they are related?" Lyra asked. She'd confessed that Tinley was an adopted wolf. Her family had taken her in when they realized she was different. I believed she was another of the white wolves of the First Peoples. Atohi, the black wolf that had tried to kill Callum, said he'd killed all the white wolves. But I'd felt the difference in her power. I'd seen her wolf. She was the ghost wolf people had seen around the town.

Tinley admitted to Lyra that she had been shifting and running at night, hoping no one had seen her, but they had. The talk of the ghost wolf had spread. I didn't feel the need to squash that particular rumor. We might be able to use it to our advantage. Not only that, I wanted to keep Tinley safe.

We were all on edge, because when someone knocked on the front door, we all jumped.

"I'll get it," Lyra said. She was standing closest to the door. She opened it and invited Malphas inside.

"Hey," I said.

"Hello. How are you?" he asked.

I stood and embraced him. "I can't hear you anymore."

"I think that thing inside of you didn't approve of the bond. The moment you shifted, I lost the connection," Malphas said.

"It wasn't the only connection it broke. Mark called because he felt the Beta bond break," I said.

"You're an Alpha," Sully said. "That's what triggered it."

Part of me wanted to reject the notion, but I pushed that back down. "Yes, I am, and yes, it did." I looked around the room and saw the approval of everyone, except Lyra who dropped her eyes. I approached her slowly, but she didn't look up. I took her face in my hands and lifted it until she met my eyes. "This is still your pack. You are still the Alpha. I won't do this without you. We have our problems, but I think it's more than just accepting my Alpha blood. It was finding a place to use it. A pack that was worthy of protecting."

"You defended me to the Martins," she said.

"Yeah. This doesn't fix anything, but I think we can work together to save this pack. We won't stop here. I won't rest until my mother and those with her are driven out of the southern packs. Will you do it with me?" I asked. Lyra needed to be reminded of her own power. She had made mistakes. She had betrayed me and ripped my heart to pieces. But she was still an Alpha female. A rare and beautiful creature. She needed a purpose and the confidence that she could do this. Had she believed in herself, she would have never sold me out. Perhaps I failed to lift her up the way I should have. She might not have my heart, but she would have my support.

"Are you sure?" she asked.

"Yes," I said.

"Then, we will do it together."

"I think that is the only way we win. Stop pretending to be together. That's an illusion too. Just because you aren't romantically involved anymore, doesn't mean you can't be a formidable team," Tinley said. She had gained her own confidence too, knowing that we accepted her for her differences. She began to sound like Callum. They had to be related.

"I think we should call a meeting of the pack down at Hector's bar. At least one person from each family," Lyra said. "We will be upfront with them. Lay it all out. Create the bond of trust."

"Let's do it."

NINETEEN

LYRA and I stood before a packed house at Hector's place. He'd provided free drinks, but we had limited the intake. We needed a sober pack, and this certainly wasn't a party. The rumor of the Rougarou had spread, and many stood in awe of me. Some that I'd made friends with kept away. I saw the fear in their eyes. I let it go, focusing on the task ahead.

Lyra explained our relationship in as much detail as she deemed necessary. I assured them that I intended to see this through. I'd even called Winnie and told her to not expect me back in Steelshore for a while. She told me that Levi had already called her. The peculiar thing was I hadn't called Levi. Somehow, he knew, and if he knew, then Grace knew.

"What about the beast?" someone asked.

"I control it now that I know it's there. It will benefit us in the fight that is coming, and I assure you it is coming," I said. "What I need to know is if you stand with us. We are an unconventional leadership, but we are facing an unconventional foe. So, will you fight with us?"

The door to the bar opened, and Henri Beaufort walked in with two hulking brutes. "I'll fight with you, Moon Dog."

Moon Dog. That was what Malphas had said.

"Thank you, Henri." I bowed my head in reverence to the alligator king.

"I brought thirty men with me to help," he said, indicating the two men standing with him. If he brought 30 men like that, I figured we had a chance.

"We stand with you," Malphas said with Echo nodding beside him.

Sully who had stood just behind me, patted my shoulder in support. Beside him Reuben nodded his head.

"Thank you, brothers."

Lyra and I waited for the pack to respond. James McCaffrey stood. "I'm in."

"Thank you, James," Lyra said.

One by one the pack stood. The ones we had trained. The ones we hadn't. The ones I'd never seen before who had come out to the meeting out of curiosity.

The door opened again, and a blond-haired, lean man walked in. My brother groaned behind me.

"I'm looking for that fucker, Nick Meyer," Callum said to the room. He scanned the room, then smiled when he saw me, but his smile fell when his eyes landed on Tinley. I knew then I was right. Callum had family. Blood family.

"Thank you all for coming," Lyra said, dismissing the assembly. Some left, but some ordered new drinks at the bar. I pushed through the crowd to Callum and hugged him.

"You okay?" I asked.

"I didn't believe you," he said.

"Is she?" I asked.

"Can I talk to her?" he asked.

I grinned. "Of course, it's why I brought you here."

"I thought you brought me for Sully," he said.

"That too, but later," I said, dragging him through the crowd. I caught Lyra's eye, and she took Tinley by the hand. We met at the back door of the bar and stepped outside together.

The loud ruckus of the crowd hushed with the door shutting. Callum stood with his eyes fixed on Tinley.

"Hi," she said.

I backed away, pulling Lyra away. "He won't hurt her."

"I know, but she's my sister. Blood or not."

"That's not changing."

Lyra leaned on me, and I didn't push her away as we watched the two white wolves study each other.

"Will you shift with me?" Callum asked.

"I don't shift much," Tinley said.

"I can tell if we are related if you shift," Callum explained.

"It's okay, Sissy. We are here," Lyra assured her.

Tinley's power swirled around her, and she turned into a pure white wolf. Callum smiled down at her. Then looked at me and nodded. He shifted and we watched the white wolves. He nuzzled her snout, and she snorted at him. Her legs and body were stiff, as he sniffed her. He barked twice at her, then she returned the bark. Lifting their heads to the sky, they howled in sync.

"I think they are related," I muttered.

"No, duh," Lyra smirked.

"Ah, there is the Lyra I know," I said. I hadn't heard her make any smart remarks for a while. I squeezed her shoulders as the wolves shifted back to human. Because they were Native American wolves, they didn't lose their clothes in the shift.

Callum embraced Tinley who cried on his shoulder. "She is my sister," Callum said. "I don't know how or why or when it happened. I don't understand it at all, but our minds are connected as wolves. I could see her past. I saw her parents. They were my parents."

"I didn't expect that," I said.

"Me neither," Lyra agreed.

"I have family," Callum said, squeezing Tinley tighter.

"Now, take her to Shady Grove. For whatever reason, my mother wants both of you. Where is Michael?" I asked.

"He didn't return after you discovered him. He won't even answer his father's calls," Callum explained. Michael's father worked in Shady Grove as a welder. He had forged weapons for the war against Winter. Michael had helped with the effort. I had to think this was separate from that. Who knew when it came to fairy witches?

Tinley pulled away from him, wiping her tears. "I don't want to go to Shady Grove. I want to stay here. We need to help them," she said.

Callum's brow furrowed. "I want to help too, but if we are the target of Araxia's game, then, we should clear out to safety not to protect ourselves, but to protect those we love."

"There is a pack there, and you will love them. Mark, the Alpha, has three sisters who are your age. You will love them," I said.

"They are a mess. I don't know how Troy and Amanda keep them contained. You would be a good influence on them," Callum said.

Tinley was still hesitant. Lyra hugged her. "I would die if something happened to you. That evil woman sells fairies, Tinley. There is no telling what she would do to you."

"I promise to let her keep me safe," Callum smirked. Tinley broke a smile.

"I've always wanted a brother," Tinley said.

"Wish granted," I said.

"Is that one of your Rougarou powers? You grant wishes?" Tinley joked.

"No, but I know a Jinn that could," I said. "It's all about who you know."

A loud howl broke our laughter. Then another. A chorus of howls filled the air as the sun sank in the west.

"They are here!" Lyra exclaimed.

"Take her. Don't stop. Can we call someone to open a portal back to Shady Grove?" I asked.

"They are all in Winter. Some mess going on there," Callum said. "Don't worry. I have her."

He shifted to wolf, and Tinley followed. They dashed off into the forest.

"I didn't say good-bye," Lyra cried out. "Tinley!"

I spun her around to look at me. "Stop! She will be fine. He will protect her with his life. We need you now."

"I can't. I need to know she's safe."

"Lyra!"

She stopped struggling against me. Sully ran out of the bar and stopped in his tracks, looking around.

"Where did he go?" he asked.

"He took Tinley and headed north to Shady Grove," I said, holding Lyra's shoulders.

"They are coming from the north," he said. He shifted into a ball of fur and dashed toward the way Callum had gone.

"Oh, god, they cut them off. Oh, no. I've lost her," Lyra muttered, losing grip.

I grabbed her face and forced her to look at me. "Lyra. I need you. Do you hear me? I need you to keep me grounded. Sully and Tinley are gone. I need to know you will bring me back."

"I can't do that. You don't trust me," she whimpered.

"I've giving you a chance to prove yourself to me. Make me trust you again," I said.

A fire ignited in her eyes. Her smell changed from a soggy morning to a blazing bonfire. Before I could stop her, she captured my lips with hers. I didn't move as she moved her lips against mine. The beast inside of me stirred with her touch. I needed her to bring me back. I accepted the kiss as a promise. I didn't return the kiss with the fire she had, but she didn't seem to care.

"I give you my oath, Dominick Meyer, to protect you and the pack of Dog River until I no longer draw breath," she said. The trees shook with the oath. It took my breath away.

Malphas landed in the tree above us, cawing loudly.

"Time to fight," I said.

TWENTY

LYRA and I walked out of the bar side by side, followed by a mass of wolves. Henri and his men joined us. Malphas and Echo flew overhead. We followed the call of the wolves who had put up the alarm.

Walking north, we came upon a line of cars that had formed across the road near the Aunt's house. James stepped up behind us.

"Your sister and Reuben stayed with the matriarchs. They've moved to the basement," he said.

"Thank you for your support," I said.

"For what it's worth, I never explained myself, but I support my Alpha. I did as she asked," he said.

I didn't care about his loyalty. He was one wolf. We had a mass of them with us. I'd kill him if he crossed me again.

"Now isn't the time for that," Lyra growled. James backed off taking his place beside Cort in the line of fighters.

"Where is Aspen?" I asked, looking around.

"No one has seen her today," a woman to my left said.

"Lyra," I said.

"It's probably her. She's always wanted the betrothal between Cort and me to be broken. She hoped you would do that," she said.

"If she is one of the witches, that is just a cover story. It goes way beyond that," I said.

"Nothing we can do about it now," she said.

Rocco and Creed stepped out in front of the force they'd brought. Another man, taller than both of them, walked up between them. I recognized him as Sirius Nashoba, the new Alpha of Orange Grove. Behind him, his Beta, Ishmael Barnabe stood. I knew where they had gotten their army. It was an army of wolves from Orange Grove. I guessed they had over taken the small insignificant pack just for this attack. Sirius walked forward.

"Give us the white wolves, and we will not burn this town to the ground," he said. Torches lit behind him one by one. The wolves behind me snarled and growled in response.

A movement along the trees behind our enemies caught my eye. A flash of pink and a wisp of rags. Willow was near. I hoped she had something to help us.

"You won't get them from us. If you want them, come and take them. We protect our own," I said.

"Show me the beast. Your mother wanted to be here to see it. After so many years of trying to produce the Rougarou, she's thrilled to know she has finally done it," Sirius said.

My mother had cursed me to this. I'd show her, because I was going to use that power to rip this man to pieces. I obliged him, allowing my anger to flow through me. I felt my claws extend. My clothes tore as my body grew. I snarled as the transformation took place.

Sirius smiled at me in awe. The men behind him

cowered. I smelled the fear of the wolves behind him. If he was a wolf spirit, then he had better hope he had brought his a-game.

I felt the beast trying to force me to attack, but I held it back. I looked down at Lyra who looked back. She nodded in assurance.

"Last chance, get out of my town!" Lyra shouted.

"Nah. I think I'll take what I came for, and if you are lucky, I'll fuck you when I'm done," he said.

That was the wrong thing to say. I couldn't hold the beast back after he threatened Lyra. Triggered.

I launched myself across the space between us, high in the air and over Sirius' head. I landed next to Rocco and with one punch, he hit the ground in a limp puddle. Creed tried to run, and I pounced on him.

"Attack!" Lyra cried out.

"Burn it down!" Sirius ordered.

I sank my claws into Creed's chest. He gasped and gurgled. The beast wanted to bite his head off, but I held back that grotesque display. Although, it would probably be enough to make even the bravest of this pack turn to run.

Through my enlarged snout, I spoke, "For Francisco and Regina. For Whiskey Chitto."

The life left his eyes, and I lifted his body up from the ground pierced by my claw. Turning to Sirius, I threw the body at him. He dodged it but smiled. "Your control was something we wondered about. It's amazing that you are still there even with the beast fully formed."

"I'm not some fucking experiment," I said.

"Oh, but you are. One of many."

A sharp pain shot through my side, and I swung around smacking the man putting a large knife in my side. He flew through the air, striking one of the vehicles. Lyra's dark grey wolf pounced on Ishmael. He shifted fighting back with her. I knew she could hold her own against him.

Looking around, I saw the Dog River pack fighting. Some of the Orange Grove minions had ignited houses but were quickly taken down by our wolves. Snarls and fur filled the air. As I focused on each fight, I felt the wolf behind it. When I connected to them mentally, their eyes glowed red to match mine. My pack. All except Lyra's which remained a bright blue, but I felt her loyalty through the mental connection of the pack.

I looked up to the clouds and released a roaring howl. The clouds parted, and a bright red moon shone down on us. Sirius looked up, and for the first moment since he arrived, he looked afraid. I'd separated him from the vehicles. He would have to shift to fight me or run, but he knew he wouldn't run far before I caught up to him.

The wolves of Dog River echoed my call to the moon. The Orange Grove wolves took the hint, and many dashed away into the darkness to retreat, leaving Sirius behind.

Bright blue lights flickered to life in the woods. They floated out of the trees with the retreating wolves following behind them mindlessly.

"Do not kill them," I ordered Dog River. Yips and barks answered my order.

Willow appeared holding her arms up at her shoulders. As she moved toward us, the blue lights moved. The feu folliet. Will o' wisps. Or as the Choctaw called them, *Hashok Okwa Hui'ga*. Spirits that would lead you astray had led the defeated wolves back to the fight. I had no intention of killing them.

Sirius, on the other hand, I wanted his blood. I launched myself at him, but instead of hitting a solid mass, I flowed through him. Once I landed on my feet, I spun around to see him. He shifted into a wolf that matched my stature and strength. Only, he wasn't fully corporeal.

"What are you?" I asked.

"I am your father, Dominick. I am the great wolf spirit. Your mother and I have tried for years to produce a son with power. You have exceeded our expectations. Look at you! You are magnificent."

I stumbled backward, shifting back to human. I felt dizzy, but someone caught me from falling. Lyra stood behind me.

"Don't let him distract you. He is still our enemy. He is destroying the packs," Lyra said.

"My father," I muttered.

"Nick, snap out of it!" Lyra yelled. The desperation, fire, and confidence in her voice struck me. I wasn't the only Alpha here, and she'd used her force to order me out of the haze.

"Pushy woman!" I snapped at her.

"Don't you forget it," she said, shoving me away from her.

I watched my father shift back to human. He held his hand out to me. "Come home with me and your mother. We will tell you our plans. Leave this weak pack and its Alpha behind."

"I am its Alpha."

"You were meant for so much more," Sirius said.

"I am home," I snarled.

"Do you know the power you have inside of you? My power. Let me show you," he said.

He turned to the wolves who had gathered around us. He pointed at one of them. I didn't know who they were when shifted. My father pulled his fist back to his body, and the wolf slid across the ground toward him. He snarled and fought him. His form flickered as he tried to shift back to human.

"Stop it!" I yelled, extending my claws.

Sirius jerked his fist, and the crack of the wolf's neck echoed through my bones. It fell limply to the ground.

"No!" a woman cried out. She flew out of the cars behind me. The body shifted from wolf to human and Aspen fell over Cort's dead body. Her red cloak flowed around her, painting the ground like blood.

"Get up. You are useless. We told you not to attach yourselves to these wolves," Sirius growled at her.

She cried over his body. I felt the pain of the pack. Grief, loss, and the fire of betrayal. They snarled around me despite the fact that my father could snap their necks. Aspen backed away from them. She slinked toward the cars, but the wolves of Dog River pushed her toward the center. I felt other wolves join them. Wolves I recognized. The Shady Grove pack had arrived.

"It is time for us to leave," Sirius said, holding his hand out for Aspen. She took it and tucked herself next to him. Her glamour fell, and I gasped. She looked like my mother.

"Araxia?"

"This is Almasta. She is your mother's sister. There are three of them. Triplets run in her family," Sirius said.

I released the Rougarou once again. Sirius shook his head.

"You killed a member of my pack."

"You cannot defeat me, Son."

I lunged again. As long as he touched Almasta, he was solid. He pushed her away but didn't blink away. Instead, his own hulking fist and claws hit me in the mid-section, breaking my attack. I stumbled back in pain but renewed my fervor. I lunged, but pivoted when he punched again, striking him in the side with my claws. All those fights in the ring in Shady Grove were paying off.

He howled in pain but planted his foot and twirled around to strike me across the jaw. Lightning shot through my head, rattling my brain.

"Don't make me destroy you!" he yelled.

"I will kill you for that!" I yelled back, pointing at Cort's body which had been surrounded by our pack.

I launched at him again, making short and fast punches to his arms and sides. He tried to deflect them, but he seemed shocked at my speed and skill.

"Nick!" Lyra's voice broke through my head and the air, shaking my concentration.

My father got another strike on my ribs. I heard something crack. I looked up to where I heard Lyra's voice. The Aunts' house was engulfed in flame.

My father taunted me. "Choose Nick. Kill me or save your sister."

I dragged myself out of my crouched position. I choose my family. Ignoring the pain, I ran into the burning house and Lyra screamed. I met Reuben in the steps to the basement. He had Suzi. He flinched when he saw me.

"It's me," I said.

"I know."

"Get her out. I'll get the Aunts."

When I reached the bottom of the stairs the women were seated in a protective circle made of silver that was embedded in the floor of the house. Embers fell around them and smoke filled the room, but they were protected in their circle.

"We are fine. Get out," Eula said.

A beam fell from the ceiling, and it landed on the circle. The protection broke. I dashed across the room to stop the beam before it hit the women. I held it up with my back. The pain caused my knees to buckle.

"Go!" I yelled.

Lyra appeared through the smoke. She helped the women move toward the stairs. She looked at me. "Come on," she said.

"Not until they are upstairs."

"This whole house is going to fall in on you!" she yelled. The smoke filled her lungs, and she began to cough. It didn't seem to affect me.

However, my body couldn't take much more as things began to fall down from above me. The Aunts made their way up the stairs slowly. James appeared with two other firefighters. He saw me and jumped the rail.

"No, get them out. Get her out!" I said, looking at Lyra who hadn't moved up the steps.

"I'll get this, and you get her out!" he yelled back.

"No. As your Alpha, I order you to get her out."

He growled at me but ran to Lyra. She screamed and reached for me, but James dragged her up the stairs, kicking and screaming.

When I felt I'd given them enough time, I rolled out from under the beam, but when I did, the fire and wood of the house rained down on me. I fought to get to the stairs which fell when I stepped on them. I looked up at the open door. I hoped I could jump to safety. However, the rest of the house came down on me, and I blacked out.

TWENTY-ONE

THE DREAMS WERE JUST as violent this time, but it was my blood that darkened the streets. My father killed me several ways as the dreams cycled.

"Nick!" Lyra's voice echoed in my head.

"I'm sorry that I failed you and the pack," I muttered to her, hoping she could hear me.

"Wake up, you fool!" she yelled.

I opened my eyes to see her and James, plus others of the pack standing over me. Lifting my hand, I saw that I'd shifted back to human. It was still dark outside.

"We put the fire out and got to you as soon as we could. Willow said she would look at your injuries," James said.

I stood with his help. My ribs hurt more than anything. Each movement blasted through my lungs, catching my breath. My body was covered in small scratches that were quickly healing.

"Thank you. But we have to make sure that Tinley and Callum made it out safely," I said.

They had lowered a ladder into the pit of what had remained of the matriarch's house. They stood at the ground level, looking down. I forced myself to climb the ladder without help. I needed to look strong, but I felt like I'd been run over by a semi. Lyra followed me. When I reached the top, I whistled.

Malphas landed in a flurry of feathers and shifted to human. "Did they make it out?"

His jaw flexed. "No."

"What!" Lyra screamed. I looked to the north and out of the smoke and fog. Figures appeared.

In the center, a tall and lean man walked with a woman clinging to his neck. Mark Maynard walked toward me, holding Tinley in his arms. Tinley, who rarely trusted anyone, had buried her face into his neck.

I staggered toward them. Lyra ran to them, taking Tinley from him. Mark smiled at the young woman who thanked him with her stare. His hand brushed over her cheek as Lyra took her away.

"Huh. There's a spark," I muttered.

"I see that," Malphas said beside me.

"Where is Sully?" I asked as Mark walked up to me.

"He's about two miles north. We couldn't get him to come with us. You should go to him," Mark said. "I'm sorry. It was either him or her."

"Is he hurt?" I asked, panicking.

"Not too bad. Just go," Mark said. I patted him on the back and ran, forgetting the pain. I had to get to my brother. I followed toward the way Mark had indicated. I came upon Sully on his knees. He banged on the trunk of a large oak with one bloody fist.

"No! I just got him. You can't have him!" he screamed at the tree.

"Sully!" I called out to him.

He rose from the ground and swayed like a drunk man. "They took him." His arm hung limply at his side. I saw the breaks in it, making him look like a disjointed doll.

"We need to get you back to a doctor," I said, holding my side.

"They took Callum. I tried to stop them, but they just disappeared into the tree. They are gone. He's gone," he said.

"Into the tree?" I asked.

"Into the Otherworld."

We had saved Tinley but lost Callum in the process. Grace was going to kill me. I'd brought her son into danger, and we had lost him. My brother looked broken. Not just his arm, but his whole spirit had darkened.

I grabbed his face and looked into his eyes. "We will get him back. I swear it." He nodded, but the hope had left his eyes. "No. You fight despair. You have always fought it. You are our light."

"We talked on the phone. This was my chance. He was my chance."

"Are you willing to fight for him?" I asked. He didn't answer. His grief had overtaken his spirit. "Hey! Answer me!" I put a little Alpha behind it.

"You are a bastard," he muttered.

"Actually, I'm not. It seems we have a living father. The real one," I said.

"What?"

"Long story. Answer my question," I pushed. I needed him to focus.

"What question?"

"Are you going to fight for Callum Fannon?" I asked.

"I would give my life for him," he said.

"Then, let's go make a plan. First point will be to survive Grace," I said.

"Oh, shit," he muttered.

We held each other up as we walked back toward Dog River. Henri showed up in a vehicle to give us a ride.

"Thank you for all of your help and support, Henri," I said as we drove back to Dog River.

"I will come whenever you call for aid, Alpha."

"As will I," I replied.

The safe houses we had created with Willow's help were filled to the brim with displaced wolves including Aggie and Eula who came out of the ordeal without a scratch. We'd taken in the surviving members of the Orange Grove pack, and they also found cots and blankets on the floors of the members of our pack.

Reuben had gotten Suzi out in plenty of time. They were resting at the Dog River Hotel. Henri took me to the bar, where Mark helped to haul me inside. They picked me up and laid me on a table. I couldn't walk. My body had given out because of my injuries.

Willow walked up to Sully and without warning, she yelled and jerked his arm. Sully screamed in pain, and I tried to move toward him, but Mark held me down. His strength surprised me. Sully shook his arm and the breaks were gone.

"Fucking witches," I muttered.

"This fucking witch is about to patch your broken body," Willow hissed.

"Don't you know not to piss off witches? Even I know that," Mark said.

"You bulking up, Kid?" I asked.

"I've been doing some working out, plus farm work," he said.

"Are you fighting?" I asked.

"No, Grace won't allow it," he replied.

"You look good. How are you?" I asked. He caught my undertone. He knew I worried about him after his decision to let Winnie go.

"I'm okay. My pack is solid and calm. I will fulfill my duties as Alpha," he said.

"And what of your heart?" I asked.

He looked across the room to Lyra who looked up at him. She held Tinley in her arms and whispered softly in her ear. Tinley had gained a brother and lost him within a few minutes. Her eyes were red from tears, but I saw that stubborn strength behind them. We needed to teach her to fight. I was sure my mother wouldn't stop until she had them both.

"What of yours?" he asked.

"It's pretty much in pieces," I huffed as Willow walked around my broken body.

"Welcome to the club," Mark said. His eyes lingered on Lyra and Tinley. Definitely a spark.

Sully pulled up a chair and sat next to me. "That crazy witch jerked my arm back into place. It's still sore, but damn, fine work."

"You will heal on your own. Nothing major," Willow said to me.

"You aren't going to fix me like him?" I asked.

"No. I can't jerk your ribs back into place. You will need rest," she said.

"I can't rest. I'm a man down," I said.

"*She* is going to kill you," Mark said as the wind picked up outside the bar.

"Don't I know it," I replied. She was near, and I could feel her.

The door of the bar flew open and the cold rush of Winter blew through with snow. The last I checked; it was still sixty degrees outside. Gloriana, Queen of Winter, walked through in a flowing ice blue dress. Her bright turquoise eyes flickered with power. The King stepped in behind her.

Their eyes landed on me.

"Dominick Meyer, where is my son?"

EPILOGUE

LEVI KEPT Grace calm while we explained what had happened. She embraced Tinley and Lyra as new members of her family. She refused to speak to me. I swore to her that I'd get him back. Sully did too. In fact, he cut his hand, offering a blood oath to the Winter throne. Grace accepted it, but other than accepting the offering, she didn't speak.

"Give her time," Levi said.

"We will get him back," I said.

"Well, now they've stepped into our realm. We will search that side. You cover the outside. I suspect they used the Otherworld as an escape, which means someone there is helping them," Levi replied.

"How are things in Winter?" I asked.

"The tensions are rising, and I don't know how much longer we can placate the sides," he admitted.

"And now this," I said.

He patted my shoulder. "You didn't do anything wrong. I'm happy that Callum has blood family in Tinley. You keep her safe. Rougarou, huh?"

"It's pretty impressive," I said, adjusting my position in the chair that Sully helped me to sit in.

"This is all tied together. We just have to arrange the pieces. Now that we know some of the players, it will be easier to track it all down," Levi said.

"Levi," Grace said.

I looked up to her. I needed her to forgive me. I still had a collar around my neck that I barely felt.

"Grace, we need to talk about your mother," I said.

"What about her? Did you find her?" she asked.

"No, but Araxia said she had two sets of triplets. She is also one of three. Almasta was hiding here with us. I suspect the third is your mother," I said.

"Third what?" she asked.

"ORC."

She pursed her lips, and I felt her power fill the room. Everyone inside reacted, cowering without moving. She took one slow step toward me. I stared into her blue eyes. She touched the collar on my neck, then reached out to Levi. He placed his hand in hers. Bright blue lines of Winter tattooed their bodies as they exchanged power. Grace's eyes glossed over and she spoke one word.

"Mine."

The collar shattered, throwing bits and pieces around the room. Thankfully, no one was struck. I released a heavy breath. The lights from Grace and Levi faded. He walked up behind her to support her. She had funneled their power to break the spell.

"Now she knows I'm coming for her," Grace snarled. Araxia would have felt the collar shatter. She would know that Grace was the only one that could do it. The combined power of the Winter crown.

"I'm sorry. I will find him," I said.

She placed her cool hand on my cheek and a tear puddled up in her left eye. "Yes, we will."

ACKNOWLEDGMENTS

I would like to thank my Patrons from my Patreon account. If you would like to join the account, search for Kimbra Swain on Patreon's site.

Faye Bonds
Denise Esh
Nicole Hogan
Paul Stansel
Jasmine Breeden
Liza Marie
Bobbie Lawson
Leslie Watts
Carlotta Woolcock
Kat HM
Ranel Capron
Samantha
Stephany Tracey
William Cawthon
Christina Yow-Barker

Thanks to my loving family whom I neglected for the holidays in order to finish this book on time. Their support of my dream overwhelms me. I am truly blessed.

Thanks to my core support group: Katy, Caitie, and Tabitha.

I love you, Jeff and Maleia.

From early in life Kimbra Swain was indoctrinated in the ways of geekdom. Raised on Star Wars, Tolkien, Superheroes, and Voltron, she found herself immersed in a world of imagination. She started writing in high school, and completed her English degree from the University of Alabama in 2003.

Her writing is influenced by a gamut of favorite authors including Jane Austen, J.R.R. Tolkien, L.M. Montgomery, Timothy Zahn, Kathy Reichs, Kevin Hearne, and Jim Butcher.

Born and raised in Alabama, Kimbra still lives there with her husband and 7 year-old daughter. When she isn't reading or writing, she plays PC games, makes jewelry, and plays with her two dogs.

Follow Kimbra on Facebook, Twitter, Instagram and Pinterest.

Join my reader group for free short stories, giveaways, Facebook live events, and publishing announcements.

Kimbra Swain's Magic and Mason Jars
www.facebook.com/groups/KSwainMagicandMasonJars

Official Website

www.kimbraswain.com

KIMBRA'S OTHER SERIES:
    Chantilly Lace
    The Path to Redemption

Made in the USA
Middletown, DE
25 May 2020